ULTIMATE BETRAYAL

By

Paula Wilkes

Cover photograph courtesy of 'Designed by Freepik'

Copyright © 2024 by Paula Wilkes

All rights reserved. This book or any portion thereof may not be reproduced or used in any manner whatsoever without the express written permission of the author, except for the use of brief quotations in a book review.

With thanks to my ever-patient husband.

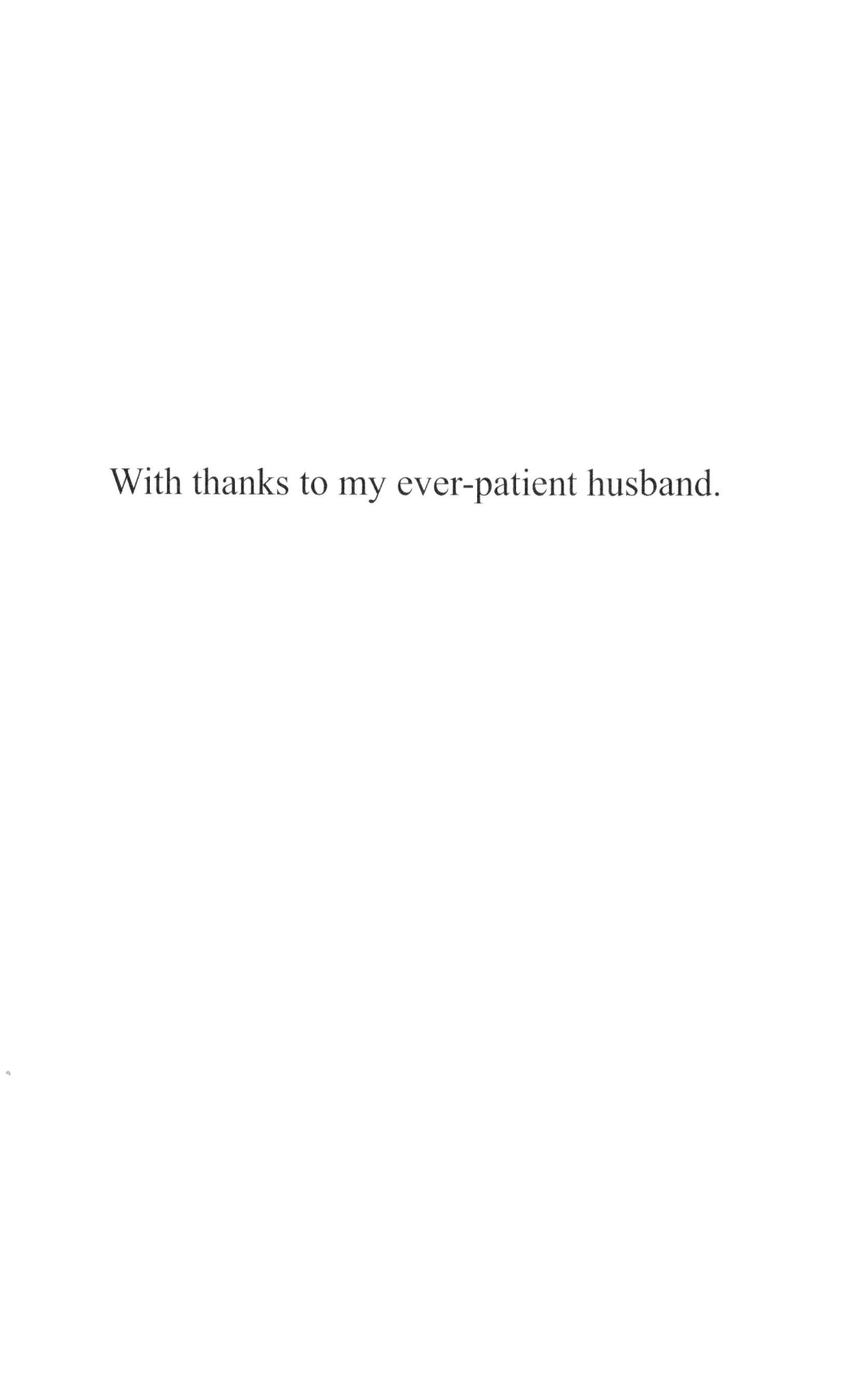

Chapter 1

On waking I stretch and instinctively reach my arm out to caress your back. For that split second I forget that you are no longer there and wonder if she rubs your back to wake you up. Hot tears start to fill my eyes, but I will not let them fall. I promised myself on the day that you left that I would not cry, a shiver runs through my body as my mind shoots back to that awful day when you told me.

We had only just come back from a lovely holiday down in Cornwall, where we had walked holding hands along leafy lanes, we had taken long beach walks across the golden sands and had enjoyed long lazy lunches in quaint Cornish pubs.

"I don't know why this is a shock to you" Steve had angrily thrown at me "you must have realised that we have nothing in common anymore!"

"But all week you've been telling me how beautiful I am and how much you love me" came my tearful reply.

"I do love you but I'm not in love with you" a stab to my heart would have been easier to take "I'm moving out, now don't start crying the sooner I go the easier it will be. I'll make sure that you have everything that you need, so you needn't worry about money."

After a few days I mustered up the courage to go and see a local solicitor that I had found in the yellow pages. I knew that Steve would use the company solicitor, who was golfing buddy of his.

I didn't contest the divorce, there seemed to be no point, if he didn't want to be with me, I might as well let him go with my dignity still intact. The divorce went through very quickly and to my surprise and Steve's horror I received more than expected. In a strange way it was my revenge watching the colour drain from his face when the judge announced the amount of the settlement. I could tell that he was trying desperately to contain the growing rage that was building up inside him.

His solicitor had argued that the company was purely based on Steve's hard work. This was absolute lie as I had been very involved within the business from the start, sending out invoices and even delivering items to customers when the drivers were too busy or on holiday.

Steve and his clever solicitor had overlooked one very important fact, that at the start of the business the company accountant had advised that I should be names as a co-director this was something to do with tax. I had just signed the paper put in front of me and hadn't given it another thought. However, this was still in force which meant that I owned half of the company. So, if he wanted me out of his life completely, he would have to buy me out.

After a great deal of huffing and puffing a settlement was reached and I walked away with a very considerable sum, plus the family home.

On leaving the court I caught sight of Steve and his new partner, as they walked across the road to his shiny sleek new jaguar. A thought sprung into my head 'a shiny sleek new jaguar and a shiny sleek new girlfriend'. He didn't look at all happy, I could see from the way that he was waving his arms about, as he always did when he hadn't got his own way, that she was going to see a very different side to her 'Sugar Daddy' that maybe she hadn't seen before.

As he turned to get into the car his eyes met mine, for a second I thought that he was going to say something, but he just scowled and got into the car.

His shiny new girlfriend turned to see what he was looking at and as our eyes met I gave her my most triumphant smile and mouthed "Good Luck, you're going to need it" to her.

She abruptly turned away but not before I had seen the pensive look on her face.

She actually wasn't what I had expected at all she looked in her late 30's a little on the plump side with short dark hair. I had imagined some young thing all legs and blond hair, I was glad that I had at last seen her.

Within half an hour of waking, hair still wet from the shower, I am sat at the kitchen table, coffee in one hand and my trusty pen in the other ready to make a start on my 'to do' list of what needs to be done today.

I find that for some reason I just can't concentrate and sit listening as the rain lashes against the window, I don't know why but everything today seems hum drum and boring.

Glancing around my kitchen for inspiration, my eyes come to rest on the colourful postcard that my dear friend Suzie sent from her home in Barbados. It must be about 20 years since she emigrated there, straight after both of her parents died. She figured that there was nothing left to keep her in England, and she wanted some adventure and more importantly some sun. So one day she closed her eyes and stuck a pin in a world map and the rest, as they say, is history.

From what she has told me during our frequent telephone conversations over the years, she had become quite an entrepreneur and now has 4 shops dotted around various Caribbean islands, selling top of the range merchandise, that she ships in from around the world.

Since my divorce she has constantly nagged me to go and visit and can't understand my reluctance to jump on a plane, I don't want to tell her that I'm afraid. I don't think that she would understand that I'm afraid to move on with my life, but also afraid not to. Since marrying Steve 30 years ago I haven't been anywhere on my own, let alone on an aeroplane to somewhere so distant and so very exotic.

"What are you waiting for?" was Suzie usual comment "come on girl, let's have some fun."

Sitting there alone in my suburban kitchen with the rain hammering down outside a thought suddenly struck me "Well what am I waiting for." I almost run out into the hall and pick up the receiver of the house phone, my fingers are trembling so badly that I have trouble dialling the number. I sit and listen as the dialling tone changes to the strange ringing of the Barbadian phone number.

After only a couple of rings a muffled voice answers "Hello"

"Hi Suzie" I try to calm the tremors in my voice and sound as cheerful as I can manage "are you okay?"

"Polly, is that you? Are you drunk?" I hear a stifled yawn.

"Oh, dear god what time is it there? Did I wake you? I'm so sorry" everything comes out in a tumble and without waiting for her to respond, "I'm coming to see you, well if you don't mind!"

"It's about 4.00 am and yes I was asleep, but you can wake me anytime with news like that." She was laughing "what has brought this on? And when are you arriving?"

"I've just decided that you're right, what the hell am I waiting for?" my legs start to shake and I sit down heavily on the stairs next to the telephone table "I need to sort out a couple of things, someone to look after the house, book a ticket and get some currency, but I should like to come as soon as possible, if that suits you?"

"To damn right it suits me, get on that plane right now!" I could tell from her voice that she was delighted. "Polly, please don't change your mind. Message me when you have your flight times and I'll meet you at the airport" after hesitating for a second she continued "Don't let anything or anyone stop you, this could be the making of you. Now go away and let me sleep, we cougars need our beauty sleep. Love you, see you soon." With that she was gone.

Chapter 2

The flight had taken slightly longer than expected and I was glad when the seatbelt sign flashed on. The couple in the seats next to me had bickered for most of the 9-hour flight, mainly due to the man wanting to order alcohol throughout the flight. Luckily I had managed to secure a set of headphones which allowed me to syphon a lot of the argument out. I was very glad when eventually after yet another whisky he fell asleep. The snoring I could put up with!

I always marvel at why as soon as the seatbelt light goes out people jump to their feet as if their lives depend on being the first to get their hand luggage down from the overhead compartments. I could never understand this urge, it seemed most prevalent in middle-aged men, who always wanted to be the first off of the plane, is this some sort of right of passage or just to prove masculinity, it will always remain a mystery to me. As everyone, who has ever flown knows you will, 9 times out of 10, have to wait at the carousel for the luggage, so why the panic.

Steve had been the same, if I didn't immediately get to my feet you would think that the world was about to end. I would be chastised like a naughty schoolgirl for letting other people off the plane before me.

Thanking the cabin crew, I step through the open aircraft door and the heat immediately hits me. Carefully making my way down the steep aeroplane steps, I'm very glad that I decided to travel in a maxi dress as the little air that there is swirls around the hem and I can feel it wafting around my legs.

Grantley Adams International Airport was very busy, and I tried to keep up with some of the other passengers that I recognised from my flight, who seemed to know where they were going. By the time we arrived at the correct luggage carousel, to my surprise it was already crammed with cases. I was extremely glad that I had chosen a quite, well for me, outrageous case with big pink and purple butterflies on it. I remember the look on the sales assistant's face when I chose this one, I'm sure that she thought 'nutty old lady' as I believe that this design was intended for a much younger cliental.

Passing through immigration and customs is always an ordeal for me. Surely I can't be the only one that always feels guilty when walking through the nothing to declare corridor. I'm never sure whether to make eye contact with the officers who man these areas or not. I always think that a hand is suddenly going to clamp down on my shoulder and I will be hauled away to answer lots of questions or I'll be locked in a secure room, with them mistakenly thinking that I am a drug smuggler or the like. So, with a pounding heart I'm very grateful when I finally walk out into the arrivals area without incident.

Quickly scanning the many smiling faces of people waiting for their loved ones, my heart sinks when I realise that Suzie isn't there waiting for me. Slowly I walk past of the other passengers getting hugs or talking to travel guides. What should I do? Searching in my bag I fish out my mobile, but when I switch it on I find that there is no signal and it just won't work. Looking through my purse I realise that I have no change for a public phone. As I look around the crowded airport a flood of emotion sweeps over me, what the hell have I done? I feel totally lost and, yes, frightened.

My mind races back to two days ago when Steve finally came to the house to collect the rest of his junk from the garage. I wasn't sure whether to tell him about my plans or not.

"I'm going away for a while" I cheerfully said, my heart was pounding so hard that I thought it might break through my chest wall.

"Right" he mumbled "you visiting your mother?" he didn't stop what he was doing, but carried on loading his car, not seeming to be at all bothered or interested.

Nonchalantly I continued "Oh goodness no! I'm off to see Suzie."

"Suzie, Suzie who?" suddenly as if he had received a blow to his head he spluttered "Suzie, Barbados Suzie?"

"I fly out tomorrow" this was said with the gay abandonment as if it was an everyday occurrence "Margaret is coming to house sit. I've told her that I have a year's visa and she's more than happy to stay indefinitely. She loves being here."

"But you can't even find your own way out of Waitrose! How will you manage in Barbados?" as if in shock he sat down heavily on the edge of the boot of his car, he suddenly started to laugh "I don't believe you. No, you're having me on."

"Steve dear" I mustered as much sarcasm as I could "why are you bothered? In case you have forgotten I am no longer your responsibility. If I get lost in transit well so what! Now have you finished, is this the last of your stuff?" when he didn't reply I continued "please take everything today, as I don't want Margaret bothered when I'm away." With that I started to turn towards the house "Oh, and Steve please close your mouth you look like you're catching flies." With a satisfied smile I walk, head held high, into the house.

"Polly, Polly" spinning around to my great relief there is Suzie hurrying towards me, her dress flying out behind her showing off her tanned legs. "Oh my god Polly I'm so sorry, I got caught up in traffic" she gives me a great big bear hug and all my worries suddenly disappear.

Holding me away from her she looks me up and down and gives a low whistle "Well my hot Momma look at you. You look great. You've lost weight and I must say you look the best that I have seen you in years. I'm going to have trouble keeping the local boys away from you!" Looking at my startled face she throws back her head and lets out an almighty laugh "Sweet Polly, you are allowed to look hot and sexy. Now come on we have a lot of catching up to do."

The drive from the airport to the outskirts of Bridgetown was a revelation, the sight of the sugar canes standing tall and proud against the beautiful cloudless sky, looked so majestic. Suzie acted like a tour guide pointing out interesting places and giving me the low down on local customs.

"Now then what is the first thing that you would like to do?" she asks above the music blaring out from her car radio.

"A shower!" looking down at my crumpled dress "and then something to eat."

"You have just travelled for nearly 9 hours and it's a shower that you want!" Laughing she added "but it's not a bad idea. Let's get you settled in and then we can walk down to PetePete's restaurant. He makes some of the best Caribbean food you will ever taste."

"PetePete's?" I query.

"Yep, his motto is the food is so good that he named his restaurant twice." She starts to sing the Frank Sinatra song New York, New York, but inserts PetePete's instead of New York, New York "Believe me he will tell you all about it when you meet him later."

Chapter 3

I let the warm water from the overhead shower wash over me. It feels good after the hours spent sitting on the plane. Lathering soap over my now lean body, I can't stop a smile from forming, at least the divorce had one positive effect as I've lost nearly 2 stone without even trying.

As I step out of the shower cubicle I catch a glimpse of my naked body in the full-length mirror on the opposite side of the bathroom. I twist this way and that to get a good look at myself, as I do I remember Suzie's comment at the airport 'Well my hot momma look at you'. Indeed, look at me!

After dressing I leave my hair loose letting the warm air dry it naturally. Normally I would blow dry and flat iron it to get rid of my natural curls. But now I don't have to worry about looking, as Steve would say, like a mad woman.

Steve always hated it when I allowed my hair to stay curly "For god's sake woman you're not a teenager. I'm not taking you out looking like a mad tinker woman. Go and straighten it!" dutifully I would do exactly what he wanted me to and spend the next half an hour straightening my hair, until he felt that I looked acceptable.

Wandering through Suzie's house I marvel at how colourful everything is. I compare it with the drab magnolia of my own house and wonder if when I get back if I could add some colour, maybe not quite as bold as Suzie's, but a little colour here and there. Suzie had explained on the journey from the airport that her home had started life as a 'Chattel House' and that the original building was completely made of wood. When she moved in she had felt that it was a bit on the small side and had decided to have an extension built on the back of the house with a porch added to the front. Her home now boasted 2 bedrooms with their own private bathrooms, the Barbadian workmen had thought this was a very typical English thing to do.

The lovely open plan kitchen/dining room was beautifully decorated with lots of local artefacts, most of which seemed to be painted in bright reds and greens with splashes of yellow.

The sitting room overlooks the garden which again is full of colour, huge red and yellow flowers stand majestically along the garden fence as if they own that space. Later I learn that these are the national flower 'The Pride of Barbados'. Everything is so very different and so exotic against my own home.

I find Suzie sitting on the swing seat on the front porch. Her tanned legs spread out in front of her. "Oh, good just in time." She says as she holds out a glass to me "this is to welcome you to my home and to a new you." Clinking my glass with hers "you look great with your hair like that, I never knew that you had curly hair."

The rum punch hits the spot and sitting next to her on the swing seat in the late afternoon sun I wonder why I hadn't done this before.

"Are you okay with everything?" Suzie looked into her glass as she asked, "you know at home!"

I gulped another mouthful of the lovely smooth run before answering her "It still feels strange cooking for one, waking up alone, not have a man about the place…"

Suzie reaches across and holds my hand "Did he leave you alright for money? Please don't think that I'm being nosy, but you put a lot of work into that company of his, not to mention the hours you slogged away at the beginning packing all of those machine bits."

I explained to her about the clever accountant and the fact that as co-director half of the company belonged to me.

"Both Steve and his lawyer looked dumbfounded when the judge made his ruling. I walked away with a very nice settlement. I didn't realise that the company was doing so well and worth so much." At this point I couldn't help but laugh "a few years ago, his solicitor advised Steve to sign over the house to me, don't ask me why. I'm sure it was some tax dodge or the like. He explained to me that it was something to do with not having too many assets in his name."

Suzie looked at me in amazement "So you walked away with the house as well?" I nodded and we both hugged each other "Ha, I bet his new fancy woman didn't like that. This really calls for another drink."

"I think that I'd rather have something to eat, if you don't mind?" Right on cue my stomach grumbled loudly, which made us both laugh.

"Right PetePete's it is then"

Chapter 4

We walk down into Bridgetown, with Suzie still acting as a tourist guide pointing out the Parliament Buildings, major banks etc. We walk along Broad Street, which is one of the main duty-free shopping areas and there on the corner she points out PetePete's.

From the name I expected PetePete's, or PP as apparently the locals call it, to be a small unassuming café/bar, how wrong was I! The restaurant wraps around the corner from Broad Street and the next road, which I think is Swan Street. The outside has red canopies over every window. These are monogrammed with two large Ps depicted in gold which seem to sparkle in the early evening sunshine.

The restaurant would rival any fine London establishment, the brass that adorns the large spotlessly clean heavy glass entrance doors shines in the sunlight and the marble floor looks as though no one has ever walked on it or as my mother would have said 'looks like you could eat your dinner of that, it's so clean'.

Walking into the foyer of the restaurant I suddenly wish that I had worn something a little classier. I'm about to say exactly that to Suzie, when a very large man with a shaved head and dressed in an immaculate cream linen suit comes hurrying towards us arms outstretched.

"Well, well, my little chicken has returned to the roost." With that he swoops Suzie up in his arms and starts to carry her through the restaurant, I trot along behind "PP has a very special table for you."

"Pete, for goodness sake put me down, people are looking" Suzie is giggling like a young schoolgirl "my friend will wonder what on earth sort of place I've brought her to!"

"Oh, chicken they're only looking because their jealous that it's you in my arms and not them" he lets out a laugh which is as deep and rich as his voice. Turning to me, with Suzie still in his arms, he gives a low whistle as he looks me up and down "Are you English? You look more like a Spanish siren" his deep laugh seems to rumble up from his belly as he speaks. Placing Suzie safely back on her feet, he rubs his chin and again slowly looks me up and down "indeed I shall call you Chiquita, my precious little one." With that he motioned to one of his waiters, who was hovering nearby "Sunny, whatever these two lovely ladies want is on the house."

Taking my hand in his he looks deep into my eyes; I felt my knees go weak and I felt butterflies had invaded my stomach "My welcome for a beautiful lady to our beautiful island." With that he kissed my hand before turning and walking out of the restaurant.

"My, oh my!" Suzie took a sip of her drink that Sunny had brought to the table "I think that you've made quite an impression on our dear PP. Never seen him quite so gooey over anyone before."

"Don't be silly. I'm sure that he's that charming to every new customer" but as I said it I felt myself blush "now come on Miss Tourism what should we eat."

Suzie recommended that I should try the traditional dish of chicken, macaroni pie and peas'n'rice. This was indeed one of the most delicious meals that I had eaten in a very long time.

After we had finished our meal we wandered arm in arm along the seafront towards the main port. I had never seen so many large boats in one place before. I especially liked the big white catamaran's that seemed, to me, to be holding court over the smaller boats anchored nearby.

We found a nice little bar and settled ourselves at an outside table to people watch, whilst sipping our rum punches through long straws. Looking at my friend as she tilts her head up to the late sun, I suddenly feel very free.

"I truly understand why you love it here so much. No one seems to expect you to behave in a certain way" taking a sip of my drink "look at me I would never have gone out to eat like this" I gesture with my free hand to my hair and down over my dress "I would have spent hours blow drying and straightening my hair, put on a knee length dress, heels and full makeup. I've only been here a few hours and I already feel different."

Suzie places her glass back on the table and takes my hand "my darling girl, that's because you have been living to someone else's beat" patting my hand she continues "you look beautiful" laughing as she tugs me to my feet "come on Chiquita let's get you home, I want to show you some of my empire in the morning."

And so, for the next 6 months my life settled into a nice little routine of accompanying Suzie on buying trips to the surrounding islands. She had lots of local ladies making the most diverse collection of clothing, from beachwear to the most beautiful evening gowns. Suzie would pay them very little money for the items, compared with what someone in England would be paid, and then the garments would be sold in one of Suzie's boutique shops for an absolute fortune.

We would either travel to the islands by speed boat or if Pete's small private plane was available we would use that. This always made me fell like some aging rock star. I imagined people trying to guess who had arrived by private plane when we landed at the various airports. But in truth I don't suppose anyone took any notice.

On days that Suzie had private meetings with either her accountant or solicitor I would occupy myself sightseeing or just enjoy a lazy day in the garden reading.

Little did I know just how quickly things would change.

Chapter 5

A loud noise in the back yard woke me from my sleep, after a while I heard Suzie's voice and she sounded very angry "What the hell do you mean no money!" she shouted.

Cautiously I crept out of bed and peeped through the slots of the blind, the scene that confronted me was horrible.

Suzie was holding a young girl by the shoulders and shaking her very forcefully whilst shouting in her face "No bloody money, don't give me that, the cruise ships are in and you're telling me you made no money" with that she pushed the young girl away from her with such force that the girl was sent flying backwards. Suzie leant over the girl, who was still on the floor, "I take it you want to stay in Bridgetown?" Suzie towered over the now obviously frightened girl her voice was almost a growl, the girl said something which I couldn't hear, but from the movement of her head I knew that she had confirmed that she wanted to stay "in that case you had better get your dumbass to work and bring me double tomorrow morning. Now get out of here, before I change my mind and send you packing," The young girl struggled to her feet and ran out of the garden as quickly as she could.

I sank down on the bed what the hell had that been about. Why would Suzie expect the girl to bring her money and why would she want to take money from her? I knew that when Suzie's parents had died that they had left her independently wealthy, so the scene that I had just witnessed didn't make any sense. I decided that I wouldn't say anything about it just yet as the whole incident had left me shaken. On hearing Suzie walking down the corridor my room I quickly got back into bed and pretended to be asleep.

"Hey, sleepy head" Suzie gently shook me, not violently like she had just shaken they young girl a moment ago "come on, up you get we have things to do and people to see." As she left the bedroom she called over her shoulder "breakfast in 15 minutes."

Walking out into the garden I was surprised to see Pete sitting at the breakfast table with Suzie, they were deep in conversation but on seeing me they both fell silent.

"Well good morning Chiquita" Pete got to his feet "did you sleep well?"

"Yes thank you" I answered as I sat down at the table "you two looked as though you were cooking something up!"

Reaching across for the cafetiere Suzie muttered "not at all we weren't sure if you were up or not, so I made Pete be quiet for a change." With this she gave a little laugh and looked at Pete for support.

"I hear that you are going to sea today" Pete countered skilfully changing the subject "if you had told me before I would have joined you." He wagged a finger at Suzie as if she was being scolded, "but I'm always the last to know what's going on" with that he pushed his chair back and stood up from the table "well it seems that I have a lot of work to do today, so I had better get on with it." Walking around to where Suzie was sitting on the opposite side of the table, be bent over and kissed Suzie on the cheek "see you girls later, try to behave yourselves."

After he had left and when I felt that the time was right, I broached the subject of what I had seen "Suzie, earlier I thought I heard shouting is everything alright?" I looked at her over the rim of my coffee cup trying to gauge her reaction.

"Shouting?" Are you sure it was here and not next door, they can be very noisy at times?" I thought that I detected a slight edge to her voice and her hand shook a little as she lifted her cup of steaming coffee to her lips.

"Your most probably right, or I may have dreamt it! I did drink rather a lot of rum last night." With that we both laughed, and I felt the tension leave the air. "So, we are going to sea, please tell me its not in a beautiful pea green boat like the owl and the pussy cat!"

Suzie threw back her head and laughed "Oh Polly you do make me laugh. It is so wonderful to have you here. But we must get a move on, Captain Tobias is a stickler for time."

As we walked back into the house I told Suzie that I wasn't sure what to wear. I was very surprised when she told me that everything that I would need would already be on the boat. Before I could ask anything else Suzie stated "Why don't you wait on the porch and enjoy the sunshine. I have a phone call that I need to make before we leave." Suzie's voice, once again, sounded to me as if she was little anxious. So, I did what I was told and went out and sat on the swing seat closing my eyes and tipping my head back to enjoy the early morning sun.

The blasting of a car horn disturbed the peace that I had been enjoying, opening my eyes I was amazed to see a white stretch limousine parked outside of Suzie's gate. At the second blast of the horn Suzie came hurtling out of the front door with a face as black as thunder.

"For god's sake Jonathon, why don't you let the whole neighbourhood know that you're here!" she scowled at him. The man muttered something under his breath. Suzie turned to face me and quickly added "Sorry Polly, but what a scene. He can never arrive anywhere quietly." She smiled sweetly at me, but I felt unnerved by all of the events of this morning.

As we walked to the car Jonathon, who was already standing at the open rear passenger door, I was surprised to hear the murmur of woman's voices from inside the vehicle. Jonathon held out his hand to help us climb in. As I got in I was surprised to see 6 young girls already seated in the car, each held a glass of champagne in their hand.

Turning to Suzie I queried "Where are we going? I thought that we were having a lazy day at sea?"

On hearing this the girls erupted into laughter "Well, I guess you may be lying down a lot" we of them answered and with that the rest hooted with laughter.

"Shut up Honey" Suzie snapped "Watch your mouth."

"Sorry, Sorry Suzie, it was only a joke" the girl that I now knew was Honey meekly replied.

A very uneasy feeling swept through my body, what the hell was going on! "Suzie, I don't think that I want to go out to sea today, maybe I'll stay here and sit in the garden and read." As I spoke I noticed, from the corner of my eye, that the girls were all looking at Suzie and back to me as if waiting for something to happen.

"Oh, don't let Honey put you off she's always saying stupid things." Suzie gave me her sweetest smile "come on it will be fine; you'll enjoy it once you're on the yacht." Pausing she continued "Chantelle pour Polly some champagne." Stroking my hand she added "I know that you will enjoy it!"

During the journey Suzie introduced me to the girls "You already know that this one is Honey" she waved a hand in the direction of a stunningly beautiful girl. She was tall with most amazing long legs that I had ever seen. I guess she got her name from her honey-coloured hair. "Then this is Chantelle" this girl was a picture of perfection she looked as though she had been airbrushed, her skin shone like silk. She had short dark hair. "These three from left to right are Christie, Princess and Belle" the first two were tall, also with legs that never seemed to end. Belle was different from the others she was shorter and a little plump. "And last but not least Tanya "the girl gave a little salute that sent the others into giggles. Tanya had an athletic body and wore her hair in a tight afro.

"Lovely to meet you all, I will try to remember your names, but I can't promise that I will get them right." I looked around the car at the six faces waiting for a reply, when none came I took a large gulp of my champagne.

The trip from the house down to the port was breathtaking and on any other day I would have been blown away by the views, but today in the claustrophobic atmosphere of the limousine and with Honey's words echoing in my head I dreaded reaching our destination.

As we entered the dock gates we were waved straight through without being asked to stop and declare the reason for our visit. I noticed that all of the other vehicles entering and exiting the port were being stopped, with some of them even being searched by armed police officers. The drivers of the other vehicles also seemed to showing their ID. A small doubt crept into my head 'why hadn't we been stopped?' However, nothing seemed to be ringing true today, so I tried to push the thought to the back of my mind.

Jonathon pulled the car to a stop alongside one of the biggest yachts in the dock, it looked more like a mini cruise ship than a yacht. After alighting from the car Suzie hurried us towards the gang plank. As I carefully negotiated the walkway I glanced up and saw a tall very tanned man pacing back and forwards on the deck above us. He seemed to be having a very animated conversation with someone on his mobile phone. As soon as he noticed that we were about to board, he quickly clicked his phone shut and walked towards us.

"Bloody hell Suzie, where the hell have you been? You should have been here half an hour ago" firstly glaring at Suzie with his hands on his hips, he then turned his attention to the rest of us. Looking each girl up and down until he got to me. "Who's this? And what the bloody hell is she wearing?"

"Please don't be rude Tobias" Suzie looked embarrassed "this is Polly I told you about her, remember my friend from England"

"Friend or not get her out of those awful clothes immediately, our guests will be here soon" with that he started to climb the stairs to the wheelhouse "and for god's sake get the rest of them ready, they look as though they've been through a hurricane."

Clapping her hands Suzie barked orders "Chantelle redo your hair, Honey makeup, Christie hair and makeup. Princess, Belle and Tanya you all look okay, get your dresses on and then get the champagne ready we can't serve it warm" turning to me "well you heard what the man said, this way." With that she walked off with me trotting behind.

"Suzie, please tell me what is going on?" I could feel the tears building in my eyes and sniffed to stop them falling.

"In here" she opened a door and there in front of us was the most sumptuous cabin that I has ever seen. The huge bed was covered in a pale mint green silk throw, that matched the curtains and as you walked across the thick carpet your feet, literally, sank into the soft pile. Next to the bed on a table was a bottle of champagne in a cooler with two crystal glasses that sparkled in the sunlight that streamed in through the large glass patio windows. Also on the table was a silver box with an exquisite pattern inlaid on the lid of mother of pearl.

Suzie had quickly walked across to the other side of the other side of the cabin, whilst pulling off the dress that she had worn for the journey. Open the large oak doors of the built-in wardrobe she now started pulling out garments from the built-in wardrobe "here put this on, this should be your size" she handed me a long cobalt blue halter neck dress "Polly, please hurry the others will be here shortly and I need to be up on deck to greet them. Where the fuck is Martha?" Grabbing the phone that was on a table that stood at the other side of the bed "Get Martha down here now" she barked into the handset before slamming it down on the cradle "Polly don't just stand there get that dress on!" Suzie pulled a beautiful purple dress over her head and gazed for a second in the full-length mirror that adorned one of the cabin walls. "That's better" she muttered.

Just as I was about to argue that until she told me what was going on an older portly woman came hurrying into the cabin. She was dressed in a maids outfit; she looked as though she should be working in a posh hotels.

"Sorry miss, I didn't know that you needed me." She sounded terrified.

"This is Polly" Suzie nodded her head in my direction "get her hair and makeup done and please make it snappy we are running very late." Smoothing down her own gown that had also been stored in the wardrobe, Suzie walked back across the cabin and headed for the door, stopping with her hand on the doorknob she looked at the terrified maid "and Martha discretion is called for, do you understand?"

Martha nodded her understanding "Please sit-down Miss Polly, would you like your hair up or down "she ran her fingers through my curls "such pretty hair perhaps down." She smiled as she answered her own question.

I did as I was asked and as she started to comb and tease my curls into place I reached forward and picked up the lovely silver box. Turning it over in my hand to see the true beauty of the mother of pearl. I noticed that Martha was watching me with a strange look on her face. "Is everything alright?" I gently asked her.

"Miss, I know that it's none of my business, but do you know what you are here for? She looked around the cabin as if she expected someone to jump out of the wardrobe.

"A party and a nice trip out to sea" was my reply "Suzie said good food and nice company. Why do you ask?"

"Open the box" Martha gestured to the lovely silver box that was still in my hand "when the girls use the cabins…" her voice went very quiet "well open it and see for yourself."

Slowly I lifted the lid unsure if I wanted to see what was inside. "Oh my god!" Was all I could say, the box was full of condoms. Snapping the lid shut I looked at Martha who was staring at my reflection in the mirror. Suddenly I felt sick and pushing Martha out of my way made a dash for the bathroom.

"Miss, miss please come out, I will be in such trouble if I don't get you ready and up on deck soon." Martha's voice trembled as she spoke, and I could tell that she was really frightened "Please come out."

Unlocking the door, I walked out of the bathroom as steadily as my legs would allow and headed back to the chair that I had just vacated. My head was whirling surely Suzie didn't expect me to 'entertain' the men that would soon be on board, just the thought of it made me feel sick. What was Suzie up to, at that moment I felt as though I didn't know this person that I called my best friend.

Seeing my worried face Martha gently spoke "Miss, don't worry I think that you are here to just make conversation with Miss Suzie's guests, just like Miss Suzie does" she paused before continuing "I don't mean to be rude, but the men that come to these parties normally like their girls to be young." She blushed as she spoke "Right you're ready, you look beautiful."

Chapter 6

Cautiously I stepped out into the sunshine. The deck at the stern of the yacht was packed with well-groomed men, they reeked of wealth. All but one, were casually dressed in well pressed shorts and polo shirts. From a glance I could tell from the cut of their clothes that they were all wearing very high-end designer wear. All of them had on the customary aviator sunglasses and huge diamond encrusted watches that glinted in the Caribbean sunshine.

To any casual onlooker this looked like your average boat party. The waiters ensuring that everyone's glass was constantly full and the men and girls laughing and chattering without, what seemed to me, to have a care in the world.

I noticed that the girls had all changed and were now in very short sexy dresses and all of them had bare feet. Their beautiful brown skin had a sheen that shone like silk, I guessed that this was through some type of oil, but the effect was breath-taking.

Suzie joined me in the doorway to the salon "I know that you must have a million questions and I promise that I will answer each one, but later. Just enjoy today." She gestured to a waiter who had been patiently waiting a few feet away. "This is Thomas, he will bring you my special concoction. Polly, listen to me, only drink what Thomas brings you" with that she handed me a glass of what I thought was champagne "it's made to look as though you have a glass of bubbly but it's really lemonade!"

After taking a sip and waiting for Thomas to move away in a low voice I asked "Suzie, please tell me that you don't expect me to 'entertain' any of these gentlemen!" I take a deep breath "I saw the contents of the box near the bed in the cabin."

"You must be mad! Of course not. We are here as chaperones for the girls. We ensure that the men stick to the rules and don't abuse these lovelies" her eyes swept across the crowd. "I'm going to introduce you to Don" she nodded at an older man sitting in the corner seat at the rear of the boats stern. "He is very observant and will fill you in on some of the details. I'm afraid that I need to circulate."

I noticed that as we approach the man, that he had pushed himself up from the semi slouched seated position that he had seemingly been enjoying. He casually draped one arm along the back of the plush white cushions that were nestled tightly together on the white leather seat. He also had on the regulation aviator sunglasses and huge watch, but he was dressed in long cream trousers, a dark blue shirt with a white and blue cravat tied neatly at his neck.

"Don, I'd like to introduce you to my friend Polly. Do you mind if I leave the two of you to talk?" Without waiting for a reply Suzie walked away.

"Well, nice to meet you Polly. Come and sit down." He gestured to the seat next to him. "We have a birds eye view of all of the activities from here. I'm told that you're from England, what part? If you couldn't guess I'm from Glasgow!"

"Nice to meet you as well Don, I'm from Somerset." I tried to keep my voice as steady as possible, but the tremor still came through.

"No need to be worried about me lassie, I'm not into all these shenanigans" he patted my hand as if to reassure me "have you an idea what' going on?"

As I confirmed that I didn't have a clue, I couldn't stop tears forming in my eyes, sniffing loudly to stop them falling I looked down at my lap so that I wouldn't have to look at the men and girls on the crowded deck.

"Didn't think so" Don leaned in closer "these girls used to walk the streets and then one of them, Honey, landed a job in Suzie's beach shop in Holetown. One day when Suzie was working in the back office at the shop doing accounts, one of Honey's old ex-customers happened to walk in and during their conversation he asked Honey is she still did tricks! Once the man had gone Suzie called Honey into the office and asked her what it was all about" Don took a sip of his champagne "Honey, was afraid that Suzie was going to sack her, but in fact she had given her boss a business idea."

"Surely if Honey had walked away from that sort of life, why would she want to go back to it?" to me this seemed like a backward step.

"Oh, my dear innocent Polly, working on the streets and doing this" he waved his hand in the direction of the party "is like two different worlds. These girls would have been turning tricks for a few dollars, but now, with the help of Suzie and her contacts, in an afternoon they can earn several thousand dollars!"

I nearly choked on my lemonade "What!" is all I could manage to splutter.

"Indeed. These gentlemen will pay mega bucks for a party like this. Both you and Suzie will walk away today with…" he stopped and scratched his chin as he seemed to be weighing up the worth of the men on the yacht "somewhere in the region of $5000"

"$5000! But I haven't done anything to earn $2500, all I've done is sit here and talk to you." I was stunned at the amount and suddenly realised how rude I must have sounded "Sorry Don, I didn't mean just talked to you." I felt that I was digging a hole for myself.

"No, my lovely lassie, you misunderstand me $5000 each" my face must have been a picture as Don started to laugh a deep throaty Scottish rumble so rich was his laugh that I couldn't help but to laugh with him.

As the sun started to slip beneath the horizon and evening approached we were all summoned into the dining room, where a lavish meal of freshly caught lobsters, was served by Thomas. Captain Tobias joined the table bearing a platter of oysters and the largest dish of black caviar that I had ever seen. The whole party seemed to be enjoying the fine wine and excellent food, and there was a lot of teasing from the girls to the men, who seemed to be lapping up the attention.

After the meal we all retired to the salon where Marcus, one of the crew members, entertained us by playing the baby grand piano. My fears from earlier had just started to disappear, maybe Martha was wrong and my whole of idea of what the girls were brought here for was nothing more than fear of the unknown.

With the champagne flowing everyone was in very high spirits and a couple of the girls got up and started to dance. The men suddenly all fell quiet as they watched with eager anticipation as the girls gyrated to the music. I had to admit that they really knew how to work their bodies, they seemed to be at one with the music.

I walked across to where Suzie was sitting on a high bar stool, we hadn't seen much of each other since she had left me with Martha in the cabin. "What time does the party wrap up? I asked as I climbed up onto the stool next to her.

"I'm afraid it's in the lap of the gods. I need to get these girls moving at this rate we'll still be here tomorrow morning." She spoke quietly "and I don't know about you, but I need my beauty sleep." With that she beckoned to Chantelle who was standing by the piano tapping her long red fingernails on the shiny piano top in time with the music.

The girl immediately started to dance and as she did she moved towards a portly gentleman who was tapping his foot to the music. Wrapping her arms around his neck she whispered something in this ear and taking his hand lead him out of the salon.

"One down five to go!" Suzie muttered.

Within seconds of Chantelle leaving the room the rest of them selected their favourite girls, leaving just Suzie, Don and me to listen to Marcus playing 'It's now or never' on the piano. On seeing Suzie stand, the music suddenly stopped, and Marcus made himself scarce.

"Well, you old bugger" this was directed at Don, as Suzie flopped down on the sofa next to him "what have you been telling my friend?"

Don raised his glass and laughed that same rich laugh from earlier "the truth and nothing but the truth my lady" with that he tugged his forelock.

"Are you shocked?" She asked as she turned to face me.

"Shocked! Bloody hell yes I'm shocked! And I could truly do with something stronger than pigging lemonade!" I looked around to see what there was "Can I have champagne now or am I still on duty?" I asked with as much sarcasm as I could muster.

Shaking her head "Still on duty, I'm afraid. Until this lot shoot their load!" Suzie waved her arm out in the direction of the salon door "hopefully with the skill of these girls it shouldn't be too long now. Tobias has already turned the yacht around so they had better get on with it or we will be the only rocking boat in the harbour." With that both Suzie and Don laughed and in unison started to sing 'rock, rock, rock your boat' seeing the two of them swaying back and forward on the sofa as if rowing a boat, I couldn't stop myself from joining in.

Once the yacht was safely moored and all of the men had been escorted to their respective cars, Suzie asked me to join her in the original cabin. On entering I couldn't believe my eyes, spread out on the bed was thousands and thousands of dollars.

In her most business-like voice Suzie issued instructions to me "Right what we have to do is count this lot." She sat down on the edge of the bed "Polly, snap out of it we need to get counting otherwise we will be here all night."

Between us it didn't take too long, sitting with our backs to the giant mirror which acted as a headboard, I exhaled and gave a small whistle "$50,000! WOW."

"Now we have to divide this up, let me see" Suzie started to mutter under her breath "$5000 for you" with that she pushed a pile of notes towards me "don't say anything Polly, this is how it is!" Turning back to the cash "$5000 for me, $5000 for Tobias, $5000 for Don…."

"Don! Don gets paid for being here?" I really was confused.

"My darling Polly, where do you think that I get the men from! I supply the girls and he supplies the men. Now where was I?" shaking her head she went over the sums again "$20,000 taken care of, right now the girls. $4000 for Honey, $3000 each for the others" tapping her finger against her temple "What have I forgotten? Oh yes, $5000 hush money to be shared between the crew members." Looking at me with a small smile on her face "That leaves $6000 in the bank." Clapping her hands she continued "That's what I call a good days work."

The girls all seemed happy with their pay and left the yacht in very good spirits and as they piled into the waiting car, we could hear their excited chatter about the shopping trips they were looking forward to.

We were the last to leave and as we walked down the gang plank I couldn't help but wonder what other surprises Suzie had in store for me. As my hand rested on the envelope of money nestled into my coat pocket an uneasy feeling crept over me.

After a very fitful night's sleep I decided that I needed to talk to Suzie about the previous days events. I found her sitting on the patio with a hot cup of coffee in her hand. She was already dressed and from what she was wearing she looked as though she was ready to out.

On seeing me she cheerfully called "hot coffee in the pot" sliding her sunglasses up onto the top of her head she added "my god Polly you look as though you need a whole pot of coffee. Whatever is the matter?"

"Yesterday, yesterday is the matter!" I spat the words out.

"Grow up for god's sake! I thought you had more about you than worrying about a little party" She almost slammed her cup down on the table "you earned $5000 for doing nothing, what the hell is the matter with you?"

"What the hell is the matter with me? What the hell is the matter with me is that I do not want to be a MADAM." I shouted the last word at her "even if it sits well with you Suzie, it sure doesn't with me!" With that I took the envelope containing the money from my dressing gown pocket and threw it at her, before storming back into the house.

Chapter 7

I decided to move into a hotel, whilst I waited for my flight back to the UK. The only seats available were in two days' time and I thought that after my confrontation with Suzie that it would be better to move out of her house. I had chosen to stay in a hotel that was just outside of Bridgetown, I didn't want to bump into Suzie, Pete or Don.

As last the day had arrived for me to leave, I was just about to climb into the taxi, which I had booked to drive me to the airport, when I heard my name being called. Turning in the direction of the voice I was surprised to see Thomas hurrying towards me.

"Miss Polly, Miss Polly wait please" by the time he reached the taxi he was out of breath and gasping for air "Miss Polly, Miss Suzie asked me to bring you this." He handed me a note. It read….

My darling Polly

I am truly sorry that our friendship has ended in this way and I hope that one day you will decide that I am not such a bad person.

I hope that you will accept this present as a thank you for your friendship.

Please don't hate me.

Love Suzie xxxxx

I felt hot tears welling up in my eyes, how I wished that things had turned out differently. Without another word I took the box that Thomas held out to me and got into the taxi.

Once safely at the airport, I opened the large white box to find the most exquisite dress. It was a deep red evening gown, with large diamante stones edging both the neckline and the hem, smaller stones glittered like little stars between the larger ones. Holding it tightly to my chest I couldn't stop the tears from falling.

The flight seemed to take forever, but at last the seatbelt light went on and we touched down in Gatwick. A huge sense of relief flooded over me; it would be good to be home.

As I followed the other passengers from my flight through the tunnel from the plane to passport control, we were asked to form a single line so that the sniffer dogs could do their job. Without hesitation I stood behind a tall man and his smaller wife, as the dog worked his way down the line. The dog sniffed the man in front of me and then moved past me, just as I was about to walk after the others the dog turned back to me and after sniffing my carryon bag again he immediately sat down. I smiled as I looked from the dog to the handler as I knew that I had nothing to worry about. Another security officer hurried forward and after a whispered conversation with the dog handler the officer turned to me.

"Please pick up your bag and follow me." His voice was pleasant, and I did as I was asked "do you have any luggage in the hold?"

"Yes" I was still smiling believing that I had nothing to worry about "just the one case, it can't be missed it has huge butterflies on it."

I followed him to the baggage carousel where we retrieved my case "This way please." At this point he was joined by a female security officer.

People started to stare at me as if I was a criminal, which made me feel very uncomfortable. Trying to make polite conversation I sweetly asked, "What seems to be the problem?"

Without answering the male officer pointed to a counter, that was situated in a secure part of the arrivals hall, "Put your case and bag up there please. If either of them are locked then please unlock them now."

Another female security officer had also joined us on our way to the secure counter and she now started going through my case. Unfolding and refolding everything as she took my items out. The male officer stepped forward when the case was empty and swabbed the inside of the case, he then walked over to a table at the far side of the space and placed the swab into a machine, after a few moments the machine beeped, and he removed the swab.

One of the female officers started to look in my carry-on bag lifting the dress, which I had carefully folded in the tissue paper from the box which I had discarded before getting onto the plane, she at last spoke "My, this is beautiful. It must have cost a small fortune?"

I was so pleased that someone had eventually spoken to me that I stammered as I answered her "It was a leaving present from my dear friend."

"Really? Well, your friend must be very rich. What does he do?" As she spoke she carefully folded the dress back into the tissue paper.

"No, not he, she" I smiled at the thought of a sugar daddy "She owns a number of boutique style shops in the Caribbean."

Another swab was taken, this time from my carry-on bag, but this time the machine made a different sound, the male officer immediately turned and looked at me "have you been in contact with any drugs whilst you have been away?"

"Certainly not!" I spluttered

"Has anyone that you know smoked or taken any drugs around you?" The female officer seemed to be looking for some reaction from me.

"No." after a pause "Well not that I know of. I went to a party but I'm sure that there weren't any drugs there. It wasn't that sort of party."

"Oh really, and what sort of party was it?" The male officer's interest seemed to have been peaked by my statement.

"It was a yacht cocktail party. The invited guests were all very well to do. Not drug takers!" I couldn't stop the indignation showing in my voice.

The officer shrugged "it's the one's that you don't think take drugs that very often are the one's that do." His statement shook me. He turned to his colleague "Get the statement chart." Turning back to me he continued "We are going to proceed with a strip search" pausing he added "with your consent, of course!"

By this time, I couldn't be bothered to argue, all I wanted to do was to go home. The two female officers escorted me into a room and instructed me to take off my clothes and hand each item to them. When I was fully naked they told me to bend over and one of them opened my bottom cheeks, after which I was told to squat. On finding nothing, I was allowed to get dressed. This whole ordeal was highly embarrassing, something that I wouldn't wish on my worst enemy.

As I walked out of the room I noticed that the male officer was in deep conversation with another man, they were both bent over my lovely evening dress and seemed to be inspecting the diamante embellishment. On seeing me they both immediately straightened up and moved away from the counter.

"Mike, I folded that dress up so carefully." One of the female officers scolded the man that I hadn't met before "I'm sorry miss, men honestly they have no idea just how delicate garments of this quality should be handled." She refolded the dress and placed it back in my carry-on. "Can this lady go now?" she addressed the man, now known as Mike, he nodded his head "Thank you for your co-operation and I apologise for any inconvenience that this has caused you."

With great relief I took my carry-on bag from the counter and pulling my large case behind me made my way out of the customs area.

Chapter 8

I had been home for about 2 months when the first parcel arrived. I remember that I was gardening when the delivery van pulled into the driveway.

"Morning, parcel for Mrs Oakley" the driver seemed in a hurry "I'll leave it here for you Mrs." he shouted across the garden at me, as he put the parcel on the porch shelf. Before I had a chance to respond, he had jumped back in his van and had quickly reversed his vehicle out of the drive.

"I'm not expecting a parcel, I bet it's for one of the neighbours." I muttered to myself as I walked across the lawn towards the house. On reaching the porch I picked up the parcel, which was quite large, inspecting the label I noticed that the postage was marked as coming from Barbados. "I suppose that I might as well have a cup of tea, whilst I open you." I said to the parcel.

After the kettle had boiled, and whilst my tea was brewing I took one of the sharp kitchen knives from the holder that stands next to the breadbin. Carefully prising off the tape that had been used to secure the parcel, I was surprised to see a neatly wrapped package with a note attached to it. This read:

Hi Polly,

I hope that you don't mind but a friend of mine asked me to send a dress over as a surprise for his wife. For this reason, he didn't want to have it sent to either his business or home address in case his wife should see it before her birthday.

I suggested that he could collect it from you. Please call him, on the number below, to let him know a convenient time for him to come.

Hope you are well.

Love Suzie xxxxx

"The bloody cheek of the woman!" I couldn't believe that after what had happened and she hadn't even bothered to find out if I had arrived home safely, that now she expected me to phone an unknown stranger and act as a bloody courier. Looking at the parcel I sighed "What can I do, you're here now. Let's phone this stupid man and get it over with."

I was about to put the receiver down when a gruff voice at the other end suddenly spoke "WHAT!" just the one word was spoken.

"Hello" I put on my poshest phone voice "Can I speak to Mr Black?"

"It depends on who you are." He spat back down the line.

"Oh, for god's sake, just get him on the phone" I couldn't stop the irritation in my voice, here was I minding my own business enjoying my garden when all of a sudden I'm expected to deal with this rude idiot. "Tell him I've got a parcel for him."

"Oh, right sorry" the voice seemed to have softened a little "this is Mr Black, sorry to be so rude but these bloody call calls drive me nuts!"

"Can you come and get this parcel today please" I didn't care about his cold calls all I wanted was to get back to my gardening.

"Yes, yes of course. Just a minute let me grab a pen and I'll jot down your address." I heard something being knocked over and him swearing before he came back on the line "okay let me have the address."

We arranged for him to come at 7.00 pm and I stated that I expected him to be punctual.

At exactly 7.00 pm a large white 4 x4 vehicle pulled into the driveway. I watched from an upstairs window as a middle-aged man got out of the driver's side and walked towards the house. I noticed that he had a marked limp, at times he seemed to almost lose his balance.

"Most probably too proud to use a walking stick." I thought to myself as I watched him stumble once more.

I slowly walked down the stairs as the front doorbell sounded, after all why should I rush. As I got to the foot of the stairs I bent down and picked up the parcel as the bell rang again.

"Here you are" I said as soon as I opened the door "Please ask Suzie not to send your parcels here in the future. If you don't want your wife to see them, I suggest that you arrange for a post office box." With that I started to shut the door.

"Suzie, who the bloody hell is Suzie?" The man's foot was jammed in the open doorway, making it impossible for me to close it "What the hell are you talking about? I don't even have a wife or know who the hell this Suzie is!"

"Whatever just don't have your parcels delivered here again. Now either get your foot out of the way or face the consequences!" with one look at my angry face he withdrew his foot and started to hobble away. "Hang on a minute" his word had just sunk into my brain "What do you mean, who the hell is Suzie? She sent you the parcel, didn't she?"

"Like I said, who the bloody hell is this Suzie? Never heard of her. Pete sent me this parcel." As he turned and started to walk away again, he called back over his shoulder "and for your information I don't have a wife or a bloody mistress."

Before I could say anything else, he had opened the back door of his vehicle and after throwing the parcel onto the back seat, he got into the drivers seat and was reversing out of the drive. Leaving me standing at my open doorway wondering just what the hell was going on.

As he drove away I noticed a black saloon car, pull out from the side road opposite my house and drive off in the same direction that he had taken. I didn't really think anything of it at the time, as this road was always very busy.

    After closing the door, I walked back down the hallway towards the sitting room. I hesitated next to the telephone table wondering if I should try to speak to Suzie to find out what was going on. I decided not to as to be honest I didn't really want to know. The parcel had been delivered and that was the end of it. Or so I thought!

Chapter 9

I had enjoyed the last couple of weeks, doing the round of garden centres and taking in a few plays at the local theatre, the parcel incident seemed a long time ago.

This particular day I had spent a good few hours at a National Trust Property, and on the way back had decided to treat myself to a Chinese takeaway. I was about to tuck into my dumplings, orange chicken, fried rice and egg rolls, the smell had been driving me crazy in the car on the way home. As I dished up my stomach mad a loud rumble that made me laugh. I suddenly thought of Steve, he would have been very angry at such a childish reaction.

The shrill sound of the phone ringing brought me sharply back to the present "If that's a cold call!" I angrily said to myself as I snatched up the receiver "YES" I almost shouted down the line.

"Whoa, someone having a bad day?" a gravelly male Scottish voice rumbled at the other end of the line. "Is this a bad time Polly?" this was followed by a familiar deep laugh.

A shiver ran down my back, as if someone had just walked over my grave. "Don? Don is that you?"

"Last time I checked. But seriously is this a bad time?" Don's voice had softened.

"Well, it is, and it isn't. Its nice to hear from you" I lied as convincingly as I could manage "I've just served up my dinner and I'm starving."

"Promise I won't keep you long" he paused as if waiting for me to object, when I kept quiet he continued "I'm in the UK, well in London actually and I would love to see you "I heard the clink of a bottle against a glass "would you be able to come up for a couple of days?"

"Um, I'm not sure if that's a good idea" I felt torn as a few days in London would be lovely, but I was wary of his motives.

Hearing the hesitation in my voice he turned on the charm "I have a penthouse suite with a magnificent view over the city" pausing for a moment "I promise to be a good boy" laughing he finished "promise no hanky panky."

"Well, why not I haven't been to London for a while and some retail therapy would do me the world of good." As soon as I had said it I wished that I could retract my statement.

"Brilliant. I'll send my driver down to collect you first thing in the morning." He genuinely sounded delighted "Oh, bring your passport, I have a private jet at my disposal so we may fancy a little jaunt." Without waiting for an answer, the line went dead.

Walking back into the kitchen the smell of my takeaway suddenly made my stomach turn. Scaping it into the kitchen bin I had a sinking feeling in the pit of my stomach, what had I just agreed to and why do I need to take my passport?

After a sleepless night I stumble around the bedroom trying to get organised. I select several outfits that are not too formal but also not to casual. As I click the locks on my suitcase I hear the crunch of car wheels on the driveway. Tentatively I peek out of my bedroom window, "Bloody hell, this is madness." I mutter under my breath, as I stare down at a gleaming black Rolls Royce. As soon as the car pulls to a stop the driver immediately jumps out, my head starts to reel as I peer at the driver "Jonathon!" I shake my head in bewilderment as I ask myself "What the hell have I agreed to?"

Slowly I make my way down the stairs to the hall as the sound of the doorbell being rung persistently rings in my ears. Plastering on what I hope is a convincing smile I unlock and then open the door. "Well, this is unexpected. How are you Jonathon?"

"Fine thank you miss and you? Are you ready for your adventure?" With that he picks up my case that is sitting at my feet "We had better get moving miss, or we'll be snarled up in the rush hour traffic." As he turns away I'm sure that I see a smirk on his young dark face.

I decide not to ask him any details, as I'm sure that I won't get a truthful answer. Instead, I settle into the fine leather upholstery and enjoy the ride. As we glide down the high street the car draws a few stares from people hurrying about their business, at which point I'm glad that the back passenger windows are blacked out. Before long we head onto the motorway and Jonathon puts his foot down as we speed towards London.

Again, for the second time in 24 hours I think of Steve, always the careful driver. Whenever we travelled on the motorway his comments would always be the same 'Look at that bloody idiot' or 'I'm doing 70 so what the hell speed is he doing' on and on he'd drone. I was always glad when we got back on the normal 'A' roads. I wonder if she feels the same way! After all the honeymoon period would now be over and perhaps she's seeing him without the rose-tinted glasses.

At some point I must have drifted off to sleep as the next thing that I am aware of is Jonathon's voice "Miss, miss" his voice sounds urgent, as I opened my eyes I realised that we were parked outside of a very swanky hotel "Miss, we're here." Holding out a gloved hand in my direction "please let me help you."

"No, just a minute" fumbling in my handbag I find my mirror "Oh dear god" I exclaimed as I saw the sight looking back at me. My hair that had been held in a perfect bun was now half out and my makeup was smudged. As quickly as I could I tidied my hair and applied some powder, smoothing down my now wrinkled dress I alighted, with as much dignity as I could muster, from the car.

"Good morning madam" the liveried doorman stepped forward and taking my suitcase from Jonathon opened the heavy steel and glass entrance door, which led into the hotel foyer. "Mr McKinter is expecting you." With that the man passed my suitcase to one of the bellhops and I was ushered to a private lift, that was discreetly positioned in the corner of the foyer.

I don't think that I have ever been in such a quiet lift, the slightest of hums emanated from the workings. Three sides of the lift were decorated with a very opulent black and gold design, whilst the other wall was completely glass.

"Good job I'm not afraid of heights" I quipped to the young bellhop who was accompanying me, but he made no reply and just gave a slight nod of his head. As we ascended the view from the lift was truly magnificent, as you could see right across the city. If I hadn't been so apprehensive about the reason for my visit, I would have genuinely enjoyed the ride. But all too soon the lift stopped, and the doors silently slid open.

"Thank goodness, you're here at last!" Don was standing in front of the lift, coffee cup in hand. "It's okay laddie" he took the case from the young bellhop "I'll see to the lady from here" placing the suitcase on the floor I noticed Don slip a couple of notes into the young man's hand. "Sorry to say this but you look a mess" he was looking me up and down as he spoke "Why don't you go and have a nice hot shower and then we can start our adventure."

"Well, nice to see you as well Don!" I was on the brink of tears this was all too much "Both you and Jonathon have called my 'little holiday' and adventure, I take it all will be explained."

"Oh, my dear girl" Don took my hands in his as he spoke "nothing to worry about, just a turn of phrase. Now go and have that shower, I don't know about you but I'm ready for some food."

Within an hour we were sitting opposite each other in a lovely little bistro that overlooked the Thames. As I watched the boats silently sweep by a thought struck me "Did Suzie ask you to contact me?"

"Yes and no" Don paused as he poured us both a glass of wine "she wants to get back in touch with you but is unsure of the reception that she'll get." He hesitated as the waiter places our food in front of us "What she does isn't so bad. If those girls had stayed on the streets they would either be dead or most probably riddled with some dreadful disease! With Suzie looking after them they have a nice income and very good medical cover" he raised his wine glass to his lips after taking a sip he added "you shouldn't think badly of her."

"Maybe or maybe not, I just think that instead of discussing the situation with me, she just assumed that I would go along with it all." I kept my eyes fixed firmly on my plate as I spoke "If she had explained it I might have reacted differently." Swallowing hard to stop a sob that was rising in my throat I meekly added "I do miss her!"

"And she misses you." Don reached across the table and covered my hand with his "just for today lets enjoy the sunshine and each other's company" lifting his glass again "let's toast friendship" dropping his voice to a near whisper "tomorrow I need to run some thoughts past you, but as I said let's just enjoy today."

Chapter 10

The smell of cooked bacon roused me from my sleep, for a moment I can't get my bearings and panic sets in, until I hear Don's voice through the partly opened bedroom door. It sounds as if he is having an argument with someone. Obviously I can only hear his side of the conversation, raising his voice I hear him saying "I know, I know but for god's sake give me some credibility for having a brain" it goes quiet, so I assume that he's talking to someone on the phone, suddenly he states, "Will you let me handle it my way" again a pause "I'll speak to you later."

I pull on my dressing gown and tie the belt around me, as I step into the large sitting room I see Don standing staring out of the glass patio window that covers one entire wall.

"Morning" I say as brightly as I can "I would say Good Morning but from the sound of your phone call maybe it isn't!"

He turns and walks over to the dining table and pulls out a chair, indicating for me to sit down "I thought that we should have a civilised full English, there's nothing like starting the day with a damn good breakfast." With that he takes a plate covered with a silver dome and puts it in front of me.

Once he has settled himself and is heartily tucking into his breakfast I broach the subject of what he wants to talk to me about. Placing his knife and fork back on his plate he leans back in his chair and sighs "Can't we just have breakfast?" Picking up his coffee cup he takes a sip of the scolding liquid "I would prefer to talk to you whilst I show you something."

"Why has everything got to be so mysterious? I push my chair away from the table and start to walk back to my bedroom. "I'll be ready in 30 minutes, and you had better be ready to start talking!"

Dead on 30 minutes I walk back into the sitting room to find Don waiting for me "the cars ready and waiting, my lady."

With that he gives a slight bow, which makes me smile. "I'm sorry if you think that I'm being mean to you, but once you we get there you will see why it's easier to do things my way."

The London traffic is worse than I had remembered, even with the congestion charge, the traffic is still bumper to bumper. Jonathon seemed to know his way around, which surprised me. He would suddenly peel out of the traffic and speed down a side road. At last, the car came to a halt outside a small mall of what looked like some very swanky shops.

Jonathon quickly got out of the car and ran around to my side to open the door for me. As I stepped out onto the pavement a man came rushing out of a nearby doorway. "Good morning, you must be Mrs McKinter."

Before I could answer Don intercepted the man "I am Mr McKinter, where is Julian? He was supposed to meet us this morning."

"I am so sorry sir; Julian sends his apologies he has been called away on family business." As the man spoke he started to fumble with the bunch of keys that he was holding "I'm Christian. Julian has given me the low down on what you are looking for. Shall we!" with that he turned and walked back towards the now empty doorway.

As we enter the shop, Christian flicks on the lights and starts talking rapidly about the desirability of the shop and the area, and how not many premises of this size come onto the market. I can see from Don's face that he is not impressed that this Julian character has stood us up.

"Look I don't mean to be rude, but can you just be quiet!" Don glares at the younger man "I don't need a lecture on the area" the young man looks as though he might cry "why don't you do something useful and go and get us all a coffee." With that he takes out his wallet and shoves a £20 note into the man's hand.

"You are bloody rude." I hiss at him, when Christian has scuttled out of the door in search of coffee "and why have you brought me to an empty shop?"

By now Don has disappeared through a door at the back of the empty space "come here" he shouts, "this is going to be perfect."

"Perfect for what?" I ask as I follow him into another empty space.

"Suzie wants to start importing some of her dresses. This location will be just right. Look at all the storage space. That room can be done out as a VIP area, to allow the more privileged some privacy."

"You've brought me to London because Suzie wants to start importing dresses!" I try to keep my voice as calm as possible "what the bloody hell has that got to do with me?"

Just as he was about to answer we hear the shop door open, "I'll talk to you after this idiot has gone" Don inclines his head to the now approaching Christian "We'll take it. Get Julian to drop the contracts off at the hotel today" taking my arm he adds "and I do mean TODAY" with that he steers mw out of the door and into the waiting car.

"Don, I really do need to know what is going on and what all of this has to do with me?" I catch Jonathon watching Don in the rear-view mirror and I'm sure that the two of them are up to no good.

"No problem" he pats my hand as if he's talking to a child "Jonathon, I think that a nice little quiet pub would do nicely for lunch. Do you know of anywhere? Jonathon just nods and we head off out of the city.

'The Quiet Woman' inn is lovely, it's set right on the banks of the river next to the lock gate with house boats tethered along the riverbank. They are all painted in bright colours and remind me of the travellers caravans, that I used to watch when I was a child, and they would come to my village when the fair was in town. Suddenly Cher's song 'Gypsy's, Tramps and Thieves' starts to play in my head. As we take our seats, next to a large picture window I wish that I could enjoy this beautiful setting, but my heart feels heavy, and the feeling of doom is rising in my stomach.

"Okay, I've kept you in the dark long enough" Don takes a slurp of his beer "the reason why I brought you to London is Suzie wants you to the CEO of her new import business, here in the UK. She needs someone that she can trust and from what she has told me you more or less ran your ex-husbands business, at least in the beginning."

"No, no I don't want to live in London and run some dress shop!" the thought of leaving my lovely house and garden makes me shudder "You can tell her to forget it!"

Holding up his hand Don continues "Now wait and listen to what I have to say. You wouldn't need to live in the city fulltime once the shop was up and running and reliable staff had been found." Pouring me another glass of wine he leaned across the table "this could be very lucrative for you. The dresses which Suzie wants to import are one off originals, unique to the fortunate ladies who would buy them. They will be sold for thousands of pounds."

"Good for Suzie" I start to protest but the look on Don's face makes me stop.

"No, not good for Suzie but good for you!" He looks out of the window as a young couple walk past arm in arm "the deal comes with a penthouse apartment and 25% of the company profits plus, of course, a very generous salary."

Our food finally arrives, but I seem to have lost my appetite and as Don tucks into his steak I just sit and look at my plate "Something doesn't seem right" I look up at Don, and again I think that I catch that same look on his face that I had seen pass between him and Jonathon in the car earlier.

Chapter 11

The next morning as I opened the bedroom curtains the sky was heavy with that horrible misty rain. The whole city seemed to have a grey cloak of doom thrown over it. Looking in the mirror to the right of the window I shudder, another sleepless night is not doing my face any favours.

Slowly I walk into the shower and let the warm water run over my body. I wish that I could wash away the feeling of foreboding that is creeping ever deeper into my brain. Pulling on a pair of cream trousers and a blue top I tie my hair up into a loose bun, which saves me from having to spend ages drying it. I seem to be doing everything in slow motion today and realise that I am in no hurry to see Don this morning. After a while I know that I cannot put it off any longer, so pulling my shoulders back I walk into the sitting room.

As I enter the room Don is already sitting at the dining table enjoying a hearty breakfast. The smell of the food makes me feel quite queasy and I opt just for a strong cup of coffee. Looking over the rim of my coffee cup at the man sitting at the opposite side of the table I sarcastically ask, "Well what surprises do you have in store for me today?"

Placing his knife and fork with a clatter back onto his now empty plate "Now that you mention it" he lifts his coffee cup to his lips and takes a gulp of his coffee "You did bring your passport with you, didn't you?"

"My passport! Yes I have it, why?" I frown at him.

"Good" he smiles "the surprise today is that we are going to see Suzie."

"What! If you think that I am flying to Barbados you have another……" I stop as he starts to laugh, that same deep Scottish laugh, that I first heard on the yacht "I don't know why you're laughing, I don't think that it's very funny."

"My dear girl, I only have a small private plane at my disposal, not a bloody jumbo jet!" he tries to stifle a laugh "of course we're not going to Barbados, but we are going to the Channel Islands. Now stop wittering and go and pack, we will be there for a few days."

Within the hour we are sitting on the runway at Gatwick waiting for our time slot. From the way that Don had described the plane I was expecting a little four-seater boneshaker, but in fact it was one of the plushest planes that I had ever flown in. The seats, 10 in all, are cream leather recliners, perfect I should imagine for longer flights. Don had told me on the way to the airport that our flight would take less than an hour, so we would be in Jersey for lunch. As soon as we are airborne Jonathon, who seemed to be acting as the steward, serves us coffee and croissants.

I look across the aisle at Don, who is tapping away on his mobile phone "Don" when he doesn't respond I almost shout "DON"

"What?" he answers still looking at his phone "Look relax, everything will become clear. Stop fretting!" he sounds annoyed and keeps frowning at the screen of his phone.

Before long we instructed to buckle up and the plane starts its descent. Looking out of the little oval window I wonder what on earth is waiting for me down there.

Stepping off of the plane I am amazed at the climate, for some reason I had expected it to be really warm, but a shiver runs down my back. Don takes hold of my arm and steers mw towards an electric cart that is waiting to take us to the arrivals building. The arrival process is very quick and as we walk out of the airport, I am glad to see that Jonathon is already standing next to a black SUV. He quickly loads our luggage in the boot, and we set off on our short journey.

The journey itself only takes half an hour and we are soon sweeping up the drive to the stone and tiled farmhouse that

Suzie has rented. The house itself is set in a beautiful garden with a little sun terrace looking out to sea. My heart skips a beat as a familiar figure walks out of the open French doors. As soon as the car comes to a halt and Jonathon has opened the door for me, Suzie rushes forward arms outstretched "Oh Polly, it's so good to see you I wasn't sure if you would come!"

I want to hold back from her, but my emotions take over and I fall into her arms "It's lovely to see you to" I whisper in her ear, holding her away from me, I continue "but I still don't know why I'm really here and why all the cloak and dagger stuff!"

Taking my hand she gently pulls me towards the house, "I thought that you would all be hungry, so I thought as a welcome to Jersey you might like to try an authentic Jersey meal." We enter the house through the open French doors and are greeted with the most wonderful smell. "This is Mrs A'Court" a little plump lady is standing at the far end of the table "she has prepared lunch of Bean Crock followed by Jersy Wonders."

Mrs A'Court beamed with pride as she muttered "Bonjour" when she noticed the blank look on our faces she added "Good Morning, I hope you had a pleasant flight." Turning to Suzie "the meal needs about another hour. Can I leave you to serve it? I need to get back." When Suzie confirmed that it was fine the woman departed with a cheery "A betot."

As soon as the meal was ready we all took our seats at the big wooden farmhouse table, the meal was absolutely sensational "Mrs A'Court certainly knows how to cook." Don mumbled between mouthfuls "I can see why you asked her to cater for the do."

"Do! What do?" I looked from Suzie to Don and back again "No-one told me anything about a do!"

"Oh, for god's sake Don, please tell me that you asked Polly to bring the dress." Don looked dumbfounded for a moment "Bloody hell, I ask you to do one little thing and you balls that up!" Suzie's eyes darted from Don to me "Sweetie, I don't suppose that by any chance you brought that lovely dress that I sent to you when you left Barbados, did you?"

"No sorry, I didn't know that there was going to be an event where I would need to look glamorous" I could feel the hostility now dancing in the air between Don and Suzie. "When is this 'do' anyway?"

"Tomorrow evening" Suzie stated flatly leaning back in her chair as she started to drum her fingers on the wooden table "Is Margaret looking after your house, Polly?" I confirmed that she was "Would you be able to phone her and ask her to give the dress to Jonathon, he could fly back and pick it up." Looking at Don "Although by rights I should make you do it!"

"Is it really that important that she wears that bloody dress, you have a few dozen up there." With that Don nodded his head towards the staircase that lead up to the first floor "I don't really want the plane going back and forward, for nothing" stopping he leaned forward "after all we don't want to arouse any unwanted attention, do we?"

Suzie let out a long sigh "I suppose that you're right, although I hate to admit it." She smiled as him "but that dress was especially beautiful." Pushing her chair back from the table she stood up and holding out her hand to me "come on, lets go outside and I'll explain about tomorrow."

"Jonothan, can you bring some wine and nibbles out to the terrace please" Suzie still holding my hand strolled towards the open French doors "Lets sit out here and enjoy the view."

As soon as we were seated she started to talk "Along with exporting some of my dresses to the UK we thought" at this she indicated herself and Don "that Jersey would be a good location, plenty of money on the island and although I concede there are some decent shops" she gave a little sniff "nothing that can hold a candle to our dresses. So, we have arranged a little cocktail party for some of the wealthiest island ladies here tomorrow evening, obviously with their husbands." Lifting her face to the late afternoon sun "the girls are flying in early tomorrow morning, and they will act as our models."

"The girls? What girls?" I felt that same uneasy feeling rise in my stomach.

"Honey and the rest. Funny they didn't need to be asked twice." Suzie laughed "especially when they knew that there would be some very, and I mean, very wealthy gentlemen on hand."

"Aren't you forgetting that their wives will be there." But this just made Suzie and Don laugh.

"My sweet, sweet Polly these girls are masters of their art. If these guys don't off load a bundle of cash on these girls then I'm going to retire!" She indicated for Jonathon to pour the wine "these poor suckers haven't seen anything as exotic or erotic as my girls in full flow, their poor wives don't stand a chance."

The girls flew in early the following morning. Jonathon drove Suzie and me to the airport to meet them, I'm not sure that Jersey had ever seen anything like it. I thought that the security men's eyes would pop out of their heads. Honey was the first to walk through arrivals, she had made sure that her long slender legs were fully on show with her ultra short mini dress just covering her curvy bottom.

Christie, Princess and Belle had all opted for knee length shorts teamed with very fitted tops that showed off their ample cleavages. The last two to emerge were Tanya and Chantelle, they were dressed almost identically in very, very short denim shorts and tiny little crop tops, the whole ensemble left little to the imagination.

I noticed Suzie smiling in a very satisfied way, and on seeing me looking at her she simply said "That's my girls. I told them to make sure that they made an entrance and as entrances go that sure as hell is one!"

We made our way slowly towards the exit, watching as the girls worked their audience. Honey was a master of the shy but come-hither look, she would single out a man and dropping her head slightly would give him the full blast of her big brown eyes from beneath her lashes. The men didn't stand a chance and you could visibly see them go weak at the knees.

Once all of us, had eventually reached the car, and were seated Jonathon slid the limousine door shut. The girls all looked at each other and suddenly started singing the Abba song 'Money, money, money.'

Laughing Chantelle waved a hand in Honey's direction "If you don't hook some decent bread girl then the world aint round!" The rest of the girls all joined in with comments back and forth between each other.

By the time we arrived back at the farmhouse the workmen had arrived and were erecting the large white marquee on the front lawn. There seemed to be people everywhere bustling in and out of the house. Local women, who I assumed were helpers of Mrs A'Court, were busy arranging huge flower displays that would adorn the entrance to the marquee and slightly smaller ones to dress the centre of the round tables where the guests would be seated to enjoy the meal and later the fashion show. As the limousine came to a halt on the gravel driveway the whole place suddenly went quiet with all eyes on the car.

"Well baby girls I think that this is the time to shine!" Honey slicked on some extra lip gloss and tossing her hair smirked "lets show these locals what glamour is all about." With that she allowed Jonathon, who was standing at the open car door, to help her step out into the sunshine. I swear that there was an audible gasp from the assembled women, as Honey straightened up and started to wiggle, on her 5-inch heels, towards the farmhouse closely followed by the other five, who were all making sure to strut their stuff.

They all reach the open French doors just as Mrs A'Court walked out with a tray of cold drinks. I honestly thought that the poor woman was going to faint! Luckily Don had walked out behind her and deftly took the tray from her, with his other hand he expertly steered the poor woman to a nearby chair.

"Well, hi sweetie" Honey bent down, making sure that the workmen had a good view of her long legs, "Sorry if we startled you. Are these drinks for us?" Mrs A'Court seemed unable to speak and just nodded.

By now Suzie had joined the group on the terrace and gently patted the older woman's arm, "I'm sure the drinks are much appreciated." Suzie pulled a chair up and sat down next to the woman "these lovelies are the models for tonight. Let me introduce you" as she announced each name the girl would do a little twirl ensuring that the workmen had a full view of their antics. "Now girls, I think that you should all retire to your rooms and get some rest. I need you all to look your best tonight." Turning to look across the lawn to where the work on the marquee had stopped, raising her voice she called across to the group of workmen, who were still staring at the girls, "and I need you lot to get on with your work."

Dutifully the girls followed Jonathon into the house and disappeared from sight. At last Mrs A'Court seemed to find her voice "Dear God, I think that you had better put the local paramedics on standby" she stood up and straightened her apron "there maybe some heart attacks tonight!" walking away she quietly muttered "I'm glad that Mr A'Court isn't coming!"

The day wore on with the sound of hammering as the installation of the marquee was finished and a wooden floor was laid. The local ladies all busied themselves with the flowers and when it was all finished it really did look beautiful.

Standing at the entrance of the marquee Suzie and I were amazed at how they had managed to do so much in such a short time. "It looks stunning better than I could have possibly hoped for." Suzie smiled as I slipped my arm through hers and added "If this doesn't ensure that you get the orders that you need, then nothing will!"

"No, my lovely, don't you mean that if we don't get the orders that we deserve." Suzie turned and hugged me, "After all you are my new CEO of the UK arm of the business" tilting her head slightly to one side "You are going to accept the offer, aren't you?" I hadn't really decided but from Suzie's attitude it seemed the decision had been made for me, so I just smiled but said nothing. Suzie obviously took this as a yes. She hugged me again and added "let's go and supervise these girls and then we can get ready ourselves."

Once everyone had been inspected and was deemed to be ready, Suzie stood in the middle of the large sitting room, "now listen all of you, I do not want any of you to be seen by our guests until the fashion show." At this she looked at each of the girls in turn "I need you to be on your best behaviour tonight. No drinking before the show." At this the whole group groaned "I mean it! If I find out that any of you have had even a tiny sip of champagne there will be trouble with a capital T and we all know what that means, don't we?" The question or threat, as that is what it was, hung in the air, "Right, now that's sorted you all have your own rack of dresses, so no dawdling between outfits. Remember the more orders we get the bigger your bonus. So, my lovelies work those bodies, but do not alienate the wives." Laughing she stated with a wink of her eye "You can do that in your own time!"

As we walked out of the sitting room, we hear the first crunch of tyres on the gravel driveway. Don, who is walking behind us, mutters "Well, here we go!"

The wine flows freely as do the orders which makes the night a huge success. The girls all work the dance floor with grace and just the right amount of sexiness thrown in. I find it hard to imagine the majority of the middle-aged and somewhat portly wives in these very slinky tight dresses, but as Suzie points out that's not our problem. If these women believe that they can look as good as the models that let them have that dream.

At the end of the night the girls all line up at the entrance of the marquee to wish our guests a safe journey home. I am surprised to see that most of the men slip the girls some money and I don't mean a note or two, but in most cases a wad of cash! Later when we are all drinking a celebratory glass of bubbly the talk turns to the money. "Bloody hell, I've made £3000 just by saying goodnight!" Princess says as she waves the money in the air. "What about the rest of you?"

Honey and Chantelle look at each other and burst out laughing, "Should we tell them? Honey buries her head in Chantelle's hair as they both rock with laughter.

"What? Come on you can't leave it like that!" Princess looks at Suzie, "Do you know what they're on about? Suzie shakes her head "come on you two, let us in on the joke?"

Chantelle wipes tears of laughter from her face and without looking at Honey and trying not to laugh again she starts to tell everyone "The old guy on table five slipped Honey a note halfway through the night." Stifling her giggles "he wants Honey and me to meet him…." Laughing she now looks at Honey sitting next to her, shaking with laughter she splutters "I can't tell them you'll have to!"

"He wants us to meet him…Oh God, for a threesome" again both girls dissolve into giggles "He's willing to pay us…" she stopped and looked around the expectant crowd "£10,000, if we will spend the night with him on his boat."

"No, I will not allow it!" at the sound of Suzie's angry voice the room falls silent "Do you hear me, I will not allow it!"

"No, you misunderstand what we are saying Suzie, we're not laughing because he wants to pay us, we're laughing because he passed the note to his wife to give to us!" Honey suddenly sounded a little frightened "We know that rules and that a threesome is absolutely not on the menu." Looking over to where Suzie was still standing with her hands on her hips and a very angry look on her face, Honey added meekly "We have no intention of meeting him; the whole idea is repulsive." Looking at Chantelle "I don't mean to be rude to you, and as beautiful as you are, a threesome no thank you!"

I was left totally mystified, they seemed to do everything else so why no threesomes? It was something that I would ask Suzie about when we were alone.

I was woken early the following morning to the sound of banging coming from the garden. Grabbing my robe, I walked across to the bedroom window as I pulled back the curtains I saw that the workmen had arrived and were now dismantling the marquee. Just as I was about to turn away from the window I saw Suzie and Don standing at the far end of the stone terrace, they seemed to be either having a row or discussing something animatedly. Suzie was standing with her hands on her hips and was leaning forward until her face was very close to Don's. I guessed from her stance that it must be a row!

Getting dressed as quickly as I could I made my way down the stairs. On reaching the ground floor I could see the two of them standing in the same place on the terrace. As I walked out into the early morning sunshine Suzie turned towards me "Thank god, someone with some sense!" I smiled as I walked towards them, as Suzie continued "Will you please tell this idiot of a man it's not a good idea!"

As I reached them Don folded his arms across his chest and very grumpily stated "Two against one that's not fair."

"Well, how do you know that I will be on Suzie's side." I looked from one to the other "is someone going to tell me what all the fuss is about."

Suzie glanced across to where the workmen were loading the parts of the marquee onto the back of a lorry and in a hushed voice stated, "He thinks that the girls should take some of these numbskull men up on their offers and I've told him that it's a really bad idea, as the whole reason for coming to Jersey is have a low key bolthole" she paused before adding "you know just in case!"

"By numbskulls I take it you mean the men from last night?" this was confirmed by a nod of her head "Well for a start I don't know if there have been any serious offers of anything, obviously discounting the stupid threesome idea."

Don pulled one of the heavy wrought iron chairs from under the table and sat down heavily on it "Several of the guests approached me and asked if the girls gave 'private shows'." He gestured in Suzie's direction "But madam here doesn't think that it's a good idea. I think that we should let the girls decide so that's where you come in."

"I'm sorry Don, but I have to agree with Suzie, the girls all have return tickets for later today and I think that they should be on that plane." He let out a loud sigh "After all it might make these gentlemen persuade their wives that a return fashion show is needed." I patted his arm and winked at him "you know this type of man is used to getting what he wants immediately, so if they have to wait up goes the anticipation and up goes the price."

Don let out one of this raucous laughs "You know you may be right" looking at Suzie he smiled "we'll make a businesswoman out of her yet!"

Suzie clapped her hands and stated, "Now that's settled breakfast is calling."

Later that day, when the girls had been dispatched back to Barbados and Suzie and I were sitting enjoying the late afternoon sun, I broach the subject with her of the 'special dresses' "Suzie, there's one thing that I don't understand" as I spoke Don joined us with Jonathon following behind him carrying a bottle of wine in one hand and a tray balanced on his other hand. "You both keep referring to some of the dresses as special, but I don't understand!"

The wine, that Jonathon had carried out, was now being poured for us and it truly did hit the spot, but I was glad that he had brought out a tray out to the table with some crackers and cheese to help soak the alcohol up. "I think that now is the time for all of the mystery to be lifted, about these special dresses." I looked from Suzie to Don "if the dress that you gave me is anything to go on and they are as lovely as that then, in my opinion, they are all special dresses."

"You're right" Suzie placed her half full glass back onto the table "as you know from what Don has already told you, I want to import some of my special dresses to the UK. We want to be able to supply the wealthy men with what they want." At this point she looked at Don "We have found that if we spray the underskirt of some of the more desirable dresses we can charge a lot more for them."

"Spray? Spray them with what?" I noticed that Don and Jonathon, who was standing in the doorway, both had that look on their faces again, a look that I didn't like.

Before Suzie could answer Don interrupted "One of the men that Honey knows has a…." he pauses and seems to be trying to think of the right words to use "a chemical company and he has come up with this idea of using a spray to enhance the longevity of materials."

"I don't understand why that is necessary, these rich woman only ever wear a dress once." This whole situation and explanation didn't quite ring true. "No, I'm sorry but there has to be more to it than what you are telling me."

"You're right" Suzie was now glaring at Don "Preserve material what a load of rubbish! She's not a fool, so don't treat her like a fool." Looking back at me she continued "he has come up with a formula to spray liquid gold onto material, so that when it gets to its destination it can be turned back into solid gold."

"But why?" I still couldn't see the point.

"You remember the dress that Mr Black collected, well that was a prototype." Suzie seemed to be studying my reaction "and it worked. Look, I know that you said that you don't want to go back to Barbados, but I think that you should see how the process works."

"Maybe, I'm being stupid but why do you need to liquefy gold just to turn it back into its solid form?" I feel so confused, is it me or has the wine addled my brain.

As this Don angrily pushed back his chair and placing both hands flat on the table he leaned into my face "For god's sake Polly don't be so thick!" with that he abruptly turned away and disappeared into the house, closely followed by Jonathon.

Chapter 12

After 2 days of Suzie's constant nagging, and once I had agreed to go back to Barbados promising that I would catch the earliest flight available, which was in 2 days' time. Suzie and Don eventually both left Jersey on their pre booked flight back to Barbados.

Two days later I find myself at the airport waiting with trepidation for my flight. Luckily, this time I was seated next to gentleman who slept for the whole journey. The flight itself went smoothly and seemed to take no time at all. As the plane wheels screeched to a halt on the runway, that same old feeling of foreboding resurfaced in my brain.

Leaving the aircraft the heat hit me and I grabbed at the metal handrail to steady myself, that familiar sick feeling was starting in my stomach, what the hell was I thinking when I agreed to come back here! On reaching the ground I follow the other passengers towards the buses that are waiting to transport everyone to the terminal. At this point I think of the trips that I had taken in the past with Steve.

He would always, and not in a quiet voice, moan 'Like being a load of cattle herded off the plane and on to these disgusting crowded buses. Jammed in with sweaty horrible irritable people' He seemed to forget that he was on of these sweaty horrible irritable people, that irony always seemed to escape him!

Once all of the normal airport formalities had been completed, baggage collection, passport control and my least favourite of all customs were complete, I am glad to see Jonathon waiting in the arrival hall for me. As soon as he see's me he quickly walks forward and taking my suitcase in one hand he steers me skilfully through the throng of newly arrived people towards the exit. Once outside he stops next to a big white SUV, opening the rear passenger door he helps me to climb in, he then walks around to the back of the SUV and after stowing my case safely in the car's boot, we speed away from the airport.

Before long we arrive at Suzie's home, we find her standing on the front porch with that sweet smile on her face, "I didn't think that you would mind staying with me" with a shrug she continues "I promise no yacht parties!"

"Its fine" I return her hug. Aa little bit of me was relieved as I really didn't want to stay in a hotel on my own, I would have too much time to think!

The house was just as I remembered it being bright, light with a welcoming feel and without thinking I found myself smiling. Suzie had already headed for the kitchen and was now bustling about. I could hear cupboards being opened and shut and the sound of chopping. For a few seconds I stood quietly in the kitchen doorway watching her, until she spoke, "Well don't just stand there, get the cook a drink."

The evening started well; we enjoyed a lovely fresh salad with was washed down with quite a few rums. I tentatively bring up the subject of the special dresses "Suzie, something has been bothering me, I need to know how you intend to get these dresses through customs without raising any suspicion that they have been…" using air quotes "doctored!"

Suzie replaced her glass on the table "We will only import a couple of the 'special dresses' a month, the rest will be legitimate just cloth dresses. The special dresses will be collected from the shop by our associates in the UK who will be acting as VIP customers."

"That's all very well, but what happens if I'm caught with these so-called special dresses in the shop." Now I really did feel frightened "it will be alright for you and Don here in the Caribbean, it will be m that's hauled off to jail!"

"That's exactly why Don wanted you to stay in total ignorance, if the worst happens and somehow our project is discovered all you would be able to confirm is that you are selling dresses. But with the knowledge that you now have if you are ever questioned it will all rest on how good a liar you are." With a half smile forming on her lips "and to be honest a liar you are not!"

"Oh, dear god Suzie, I know when I got divorced that I wanted a bit of excitement, but I never thought for a moment that coming here for a holiday would first make me a madam and now an accomplice to gold smuggling" at this point I didn't know whether to laugh or cry!

Before retiring to bed and a much need sleep, Suzie had told me that we would be travelling to one of her most remote warehouses in the morning, so that I could see for myself what she called her little project.

The following day was another hot one. I had dressed in a maxi dress and sandals with my hair tied up in a high ponytail. As I walked through the house I could hear Suzie talking to someone on the front porch, their voices sounded quite hostile "I don't know what you think that you will gain from this" a man's voice drifted through the open window to the left of the front door.

"If she can see it for herself she won't be so scared" it was obvious that Suzie and this man were talking about me "If she thinks that she knows the process all will be good." That phrase from Suzie would circle in my brain in the months to come.

I creep back into the kitchen and start clattering cups to make it look as though I have just got up. After a few minutes Suzie comes into the house. "I'm sorry no time for breakfast, we need to get going" turning towards the front door she adds "I'll get Jonathon to stop on route and get us coffee."

The roads leading to the warehouse are narrow and bumpy and not for the first time I am glad that Suzie likes to travel in style. Looking out of the car window I suddenly think of Steve and what he would say about my situation.

"You a CEO of a company you must be joking. What do you know about business?"

He always conveniently forgot how much I had contributed to the company when he first started out. In fact, I was surprised that I seemed to know more about planning and cash flow than he did. True he was the engineer who knew all about parts but that alone doesn't make a good company. As our divorce proved. I wonder if she has a good head for business.

Suzie's voice brings me back to the present "We're here" she says as she gets out of the car and turns her face to me "Now Polly, do not ask any of the workers any questions. Store them up and I will tell you everything that you need to know when we leave." Her face is set in a stern mask "Do you understand?" I dutifully nod and we make our way into the warehouse.

Although the building is enormous it is completely shielded from the nearby road by tall trees and thick shrubs, in fact you would drive right by without even knowing that it was there.

The inside of the building is divided into several areas. One has machinists all of which are hunched over their sewing machines, the needles going at breakneck speed. There are wooden crates on the floor next to each machinist that seem to be full of dresses waiting to be sewn together. On the other side of each worker are open shelves holding boxes of beads and crystals, each box has a picture of its contents displayed on the outside depicting exactly what colour and size of beads are inside. Beyond the shelves a woman is meticulously inspecting finished dresses, snipping off stray strands of cotton and then placing them on wooden stands. In this area there are what looks like large steam machines, another worker is carefully steaming the garments, whilst a third woman folds and places them in blue boxes.

The second area seems to be a cutting room, bales of different coloured bales of very expensive looking cloth are stacked on shelves that reach from the floor to the warehouse ceiling. There are two men at each bench who are using various tools to cut and shape the material that is spread out on their work benches.

The last area is accessed through a heavy steel door. I'm surprised to see that two very big muscular guards are positioned in front of this door and only move aside when they recognise Suzie. I again get a feeling of foreboding that sends a shiver down my spine. Not for the last time will I wonder what the hell I am doing here.

As we walk beyond the heavy steel door we enter a narrow, but brightly lit corridor, with brick walls running the length of this part of the building. On each side of the corridor a huge glass window is set into the thick brick walls. Through the window on the left-hand side of the corridor, I see six figures all dressed from head to toe in white suits, like the one's that detectives wear on TV when they are at a crime scene, each figure is unrecognisable as being either male or female due to the full respiratory face mask they are wearing. Clothes hangers with underskirts are hung on racks that seems to come in from the first area of the building and then travel around this room. The white suited individuals are each spraying, what I assume is the liquid gold, onto each garment as it stops in front of them.

Through the window on the right-hand side of the corridor I see people, mostly woman, sewing the underskirts into dresses. The same scenario is taking place in this area, as in the first one that we passed through on entering the building, with a woman inspecting each finished dress and then a steaming process and finally wrapping. The only difference in this area is that each dress once folded is placed into a black box. I want to ask Suzie why these woman are also wearing the suits and respiratory masks but remember that no questions are to be asked within the confines of the building.

As I look through the window at the woman I suddenly notice a burly bored looking guard sitting in the corner of the room. He seems to be playing some sort of game on his mobile phone and is oblivious to anything that is happening in the room. The look on Suzie's face as observes him, tells me that she is not pleased, and I half expect her to barge into the room and give him a good roasting. But she turns abruptly away from the window, and we continue our tour. It seems strange to me that since entering the building not one person has spoken or looked at us, other than the whirl of the machinery the place is dead quiet.

At the end of the corridor is another huge steel door, but to my surprise we do not enter. As we get closer a strange smell hits my nostrils, I know that Suzie has smelt it as well as she quickly turns and marches me back along the corridor and out into the first area.

"Polly I need to do something; would you mind waiting in the car for a moment?" as she pushes me gently towards the exit she beckons to Jonathon to join her, and they both disappear back through the steel door and walk back into the corridor.

After what seems like hours Suzie and Jonathon, along with another man that I haven't seen before, walk out into the sunshine. I can tell from Suzie's body language that she is not happy with the man. She keep gesturing towards the building, as their animated conversation continues the man's whole demeanour changes and by the end of the discussion he looks totally crushed. After one last wag of her finger at him Suzie turns away and starts to walk towards the car with Jonathon close on her heels.

As she climbs into the back seat next to me I tentatively ask, "Is everything alright?"

"It will be when that bloody fool gets his act together." She nods her head towards the man who is still standing outside of the building. "Call himself a manager! If he doesn't get his act together and quickly the only thing he'll be good for is fish food."

    Little did I know at the time that this statement would come back to haunt me!

Chapter 13

The next couple of weeks fly by in a whirl of activity. I arrived back in London to find that the work on the shop was well underway. The place looked fantastic, the inside had been designed with black and chrome hanging spaces, which made this area look very expensive and stylish. Positioned down the centre of this section of the shop was a long black highly polished table, that would be used to display the accessories that the customers would need to complete their outfits.

The VIP area was exceptionally plush, with big cream sofa's that were covered in huge cushions. In the corner was a small bar with shelves behind that were ready to be stocked with the finest champagne and crystal ware. A small fridge had been installed to the right of the bar and Don informed me that this was to hold the best caviar, he had placed an order with one of the top stores to ensure that fresh caviar would be delivered at a moment's notice.

The day that I had arrived back Don, who had been in London for the past week, informed me that he had arranged for several girls to some to the shop for interviews. From the way that he was talking about the individual candidates, I suspected that he must already have known them, most probably through his London associates. Later that afternoon, Don and I waited in the shop for these ladies to show up. Unsurprisingly one after another, they trooped in on their six-inch-high heels, which collectively I would refer to them as Barbie clones, plastic pretty, with long legs, long hair and big surgically enhanced breasts. However, I had to concede that pretty girls did very often bring in customer and this would enhance our sells. So, I bowed to Don's wish and said that I would give them a fair try.

I quickly settled into a routine of staying at my very swanky penthouse form Monday to Friday, and then travelling back down to Somerset for the weekends. This seemed to be working fine whilst the shop was still under construction, but I was beginning to think that it may not work once the shop was fully up and running.

After speaking to the Barbie Clones on an individual basis none of them seemed to have any brain cells and I knew that I would not be able to put any of them in charge, when I wasn't there. I broached this subject with Don and told him that I needed an assistant manager who had a brain and was maybe slightly older who could step in and be in charge in my absence.

It was a rainy Monday morning and my taxi had been late picking me up, the traffic was horrendous. After sitting in a bumper-to-bumper jam for nearly half an hour, I decided to get out and walk the finale mile. I'd forgotten that I had on four-inch heels and before long my feet were complaining. As luck would have it I was right outside of a coffee shop and on entering I ordered a flat white, turning to survey the scene I noticed that all of the tables were already taken.

However, in the far corner of the café sitting all alone was an older lady. Cautiously weaving my way past prams and discarded umbrellas I approached her, "Excuse me, do you mind if I join you?" she looked up and nodded "everyone seems to have the same idea today." I took out my phone and started texting Don to tell him I would be in later.

"Are you late for work?" she spoke in a soft accent, that I couldn't place.

"Just letting them know that I'll be in later." For the first time I looked directly at her, she looked sad and if I wasn't mistaken had been crying, "are you alright?"

"Oh yes," looking down into her nearly empty coffee cup "just another rejection this morning. Everyone wants young people even though they have no experience, employers seem to think that if you are over 50 you should lie down and die!" her eyes shot up to meet mine, "Sorry, sorry just needed to get that off my chest."

"No problem, sometimes it's easier to speak to a stranger" I smile at her, there was something about her that I liked, maybe her honesty "what type of jobs have you been looking for?" looking at her sitting there in her shabby coat, which had obviously seen better days, I thought maybe house cleaner or waitressing, something along those lines.

"I used to be a department manager in the big Briggs store that closed down last year." She runs her hand down over her coat "although to look at me now you'd never think it!"

"Do you have references?" my heart was in my mouth as I watched her fumble in her bag and bring out several pieces of paper. "Do you mind if I look at those?" she handed them over without a word. My eyes flicked over her CV which told me that her name was Marie Martinez, 10 'O' levels, 4 'A' levels, a letter from her last employer describing her as an exemplary employee of 20 years. All of the time that I had been reading her documents I could feel her eyes on me. Finally looking up and without hesitation I stated "Marie, the rain this morning must have been heaven sent!"

"I don't understand. Heaven sent?" Her eyes searched my face.

"I would like to offer you a job." At that moment I think that we could have both cried "I'm opening a very exclusive dress shop, just down the road at the Royal Mall and I need someone with a brain to help me run it."

"Do you mean it? You would employ me even with me looking like this?" Her voice was low as if she was fighting to hold back her tears.

"Even with you looking as you do." I stop and smile at her "But we will have to smarten you up" cringing inside I continue "sorry that sounded very blunt."

"Sound as blunt as you like, if there's a job at the end of it I don't mind." She looked past me and out of the window "heaven sent, yes the rain was definitely heaven sent!"

After further discussions which resulted in me giving her £500 to get her hair done and to buy a nice smart black dress, as I wanted all of the staff to wear black, this didn't go down too well with the Barbie Clones, as apparently it doesn't enhance their eye colour or some such nonsense. I leave her with the understanding that she will be at the shop at 10.00 am the following morning. Walking out of the coffee shop the rain has stopped and I start to wonder what Don will say about me picking up my under manager without his say so, "Oh well too bad" I get a funny look from a man who is walking past me, as I must have said that out loud and not, as intended, in my head.

A week or so later during one of our meetings to discuss how the shop would operate with the Barbie clones, and who would be responsible for what, Jemma one of the more together clones tentatively asked "But what's it called? The shop what's the name of the shop? We keep calling it 'The Shop' but it has to have a name!"

Don, Marie and I all looked at each other in total silence, "You have a very good point there Jemma" Don smiled one of his special smiles at the now beaming girl "How about a suggestion from everyone and we" he indicated to the three of us "will chose a winner."

The clones all chimed in with ideas such as 'Babes do dresses', 'Royal Dresses', 'Bling is the thing' and so on. In desperation I brought the session to an end as I added "All of these are good ideas" adding 'Not' in my head, "but I thought that as all of you and Marie were, in my opinion, heaven sent why not call the shop 'Heaven Sent'" to my surprise everyone thought that this was a great idea and so 'Heaven Sent' was born.

After months of waiting the shop was finally ready to open and a Grand Opening Night had been arranged. Black and Gold invitations had all been hand delivered to the wealthiest families in the area announcing the event and much to our great delight all but one invitation had been accepted.

The Barbie Clones were ecstatic at the thought of putting on a fashion show for the wealthy local ladies and their enormously wealthy husbands. At dead on 9.00 pm, on the night of the event, the cars started to arrive in a line of very shiny limousines each with their livered chauffer, bringing the crème de la crème to our shop door.

The night started off slowly with chit chat between the ladies and the men eyeing up the Barbies. The men reminded me of the one's that had attended the yacht party. All of them were dressed in very expensive tuxedos with diamond cufflinks that glittered under the crystal chandelier. They all exuded power and wealth, and I instinctively knew that given half the chance they would rather be taking on of the Barbie's home with after the event, than their older demanding wives.

At exactly 11.00 pm Don switched on the microphone and announced that the fashion show would be commencing in 10 minutes. The gold and satin cushioned chairs that lined either side of the temporary catwalk were soon full and with the help of the fine champagne and caviar everyone seemed to be ready to spend, spend, spend.

It was 2.00 am when the last of the guests left and I finally handed a glass of bubbly, and we drink to a very successful night. Most of the dresses that were shown had been sold and orders for a variety of different colours in the styles had been taken. Earlier when we had quickly totted up the deposits on the orders it came to approximately £100,000, but the finally total, once the dresses had been made, the final total would be nearer to £300,000. Marie gave a low whistle "I can't believe how much these people are willing to pay for a dress!"

The next day the first of the 'special dresses' arrived, the Barbie's had all been given strict instructions that any dress delivered in a black clothes bag was to be given immediately to Marie or myself. The only dresses that were to be put in the stock room or displayed would always be delivered in blue bags. Marie never questioned why these were special and it wasn't until much later that I found out why.

It was a few days later when our first VIP customer entered the shop. He was well over six feet tall and had the physic of a basketball player, this large diamond earring sparkled against his dark skin. The Barbie's were almost beside themselves. Marie quickly walked forward and after a short greeting, much to the consternation of the hair flicking girls, whisked him into the discrete VIP area. I joined them and after checking his ID, something that Don had insisted on he confirmed that he didn't need to look at the dress. Reaching into his inside pocket of this leather jacket he handed over a huge wad of cash and as this happened I saw a flicker of confusion cross Marie's face, but she just handed the black bag containing the dress to him and he was gone.

At the beginning a black bag would arrive every two or three weeks, which resulted in the same type of exchange. But before long the deliveries started coming every week. On one of my regular calls with Suzie, I mentioned that I thought the deliveries were becoming too frequent, but she just laughed and said that it was fine. Little did I know that this conversation would come back to haunt me in the near future.

Chapter 14

Driving out of London towards Somerset, not for the first time do I remind myself how lucky I was to stumble across Marie in that coffee, she is an absolute treasure. Nothing gets past her, the Barbies are now all wearing smart knee length black dresses with minimum makeup and actually seem to be learning how to act and sound professional.

The shop has been so busy that we are now thinking of extending the opening times. The ladies who lunch have become regulars and very often buy two or three dresses at a time, much to Don's delight. The only fly in the ointment is the weekly delivery of the 'special dresses'.

Before I know it I am turning the car into my driveway, a wave of happiness spreads over me as I love this place. Swinging my weekend bag out of the boot I almost skip to the front door, I'm that happy to be home. As I unlock the door I notice that a parcel has been pushed behind the flowerpots that stand on the porch floor, after picking it up I turn it over and notice that it has a Barbados postmark. "What the hell" I mutter to myself as I step over the threshold and into the hallway.

I drop my weekend bag on the hall floor and walking through to the kitchen, I place the parcel on the wooden kitchen table.

Crossing to the sink I fill the kettle whilst looking out onto the garden, at this time of year it's in full colour with the climbing roses and the majestic rhododendrons all in full bloom. My ritual after the long drive home is always to wander around the garden whilst I enjoy a nice I cup of tea.

Today curiosity gets the better of me, and after selecting a sharp kitchen knife from the cutlery draw I slice open the brown paper wrapping, there inside is a carefully folded parcel secured in a black clothes bag with a note attached: -

Hi Polly

Sorry to do this to you, but Mr Black can only collect his parcel from you in Somerset. Don't be mad! Give him a call and he will immediately collect it.

Love

Suzie xx

"Oh, bloody hell Suzie" I am absolutely livid as I really don't want that man at my home again "this had better be the last time." I mutter to myself.

I tap the phone number into my mobile phone and as soon as it rings it is answered, without waiting or allowing any of the normal pleasantries I hiss down the phone "I have your parcel, please come and pick it up NOW!" without giving him a chance to answer I finish the call. Without thinking I screw the note up and throw it into the kitchen bin.

Within half an hour I hear the crunch of car tyres on the gravel driveway, not wanting him to come into the house I grab the parcel and race out to his car. Thrusting the parcel at him through the open driver's side door and in the sternest voice, that I can manage I tell him "Please make other arrangements, I do not want parcels sent to my home." The look on his face was one of complete surprise. Without a word he takes the parcel and slams his car door shut. I give a sigh of relief as he zooms off out of the driveway. "Thank god, now perhaps I can enjoy my days off!"

A hammering on the front door startles me from my sleep. Looking at the clock, which stood on my bedside cabinet I could see that it was 2.30 am. I jumped as the hammering started again and I could hear various voices shouting. Quickly I got out of bed and hurriedly open the bedroom window. I was not prepared for what I saw.

"Up there Sarg. Someone at the window." A uniformed police officer is pointing at me.

"What's going on? I stammered still half asleep.

"Mrs Oakley, please open the door." A man in a dark suit stepped out of the shadow of the house as he spoke.

I almost fell down the stairs in my haste and was trembling both with shock and fright as I unlocked the front door. As soon as the door was opened some police officers came racing in, some headed straight for the staircase and ran up to the first floor, whilst others headed for the downstairs rooms.

Finding my voice I shouted "Will someone please tell me what the hell is going on? Turning I come face to face with the man in the dark suit, "you wake me up at this ungodly hour and without another word I have people all over my house. What do you want?"

Taking my arm, he led me into the sitting room "Please sit down" looking over my shoulder at a young policewoman he continued "I think that Mrs Oakley could do with a cup of tea."

"Cup of tea, more like a bloody brandy!" what was happening to me.

"Mrs Oakley, please try to concentrate. I know that this has come as a shock, and I am sorry that we have burst into your home at this 'ungodly hour' but we need to ensure that no-one else is in the house." He stopped as the policewoman brought in a tray with two mugs of tea and a plate of biscuits on it. "I am Detective Chief Inspector Mark Wilson; I am over the drug squad for the Southwest of England." With that he handed me a mug of tea.

"Drug Squad?" my head is reeling, "I don't take or have anything to do with drugs. So why are you here in my home?" I took a sip of the scolding hot tea, "please tell me that this is some terrible mistake!"

The police officer who had pointed to me at the bedroom window stepped into the room. "Nothing sir, the house is clear."

"Thank you." Mark Wilson looked back at me "you need to get dressed; PC Bennet will accompany you."

"But he's just said that the house is clear, so why do I need to get dressed?" I looked at the young PC who was standing behind the chair that Mark Wilson was sitting in "I really don't understand. Please tell me that this is a bad dream."

"Unfortunately, you are very much awake. You need to come to the station with me, so I suggest that you get dressed." He placed his mug back onto the tray and nodded to the female PC "Please take Mrs Oakley upstairs. I'm going back to the station." With that he stood up and walked out of the house.

After reluctantly getting dressed I was put in a marked police car and driven at speed to the police station. On arrival I was led down a long corridor and shown into a windowless room. The policewoman pointed to a hard plastic chair on the far side of a Formica table "Please sit there Mrs Oakley." With that she turned to walk out of the room.

"Please wait. I don't understand what is going on." I pleaded with her "why am I here?"

"DCI Wilson will be with you shortly." Came the gruff reply, with that she walked out and slammed the door behind her.

A sudden wave of nausea came over, me as I took in my surroundings. The room contained just the Formica table, which didn't look particularly clean, and four had plastic chairs, one of which I was sitting on. The room was really scruffy with a single fairly large light in the centre of the ceiling, which was covered with some sort of cage. In the corner of the room to the right of the door I noticed what looked like a CCTV camera. I shuddered wondering if someone was sitting on the other side of the camera watching me.

At last, the door opened and in walked DCI Wilson, accompanied by another man who introduced himself as DS Brian Hurford. The two detectives took their seats on the opposite side of the table.

"Well, is anyone going to tell me what this is all about! You come barging into my home, drag me down here to this.." I wave my hand around the scruffy room "leave me sitting in this filthy cold room for ages, for what?...."

I was just getting into my stride when DCI Wilson held up his hand "Well if you give me a minute….."

"Give you a minute!" I angrily interrupt him "I've already given you two hours!"

"As I was about to say" he continued "we understand that you received a parcel yesterday."

"What! All of this is about a parcel!" Now I am really confused "the parcel wasn't even for me. If you want that parcel why come to my home, why didn't you barge into Mr Black's home and wake him up, instead of me?"

Both detectives had started to make notes in their big black notebooks, "Mr Black, you say that the parcel was addressed to a Mr Black?" Brian Hurford muttered something without looking up from his notebook, when I didn't answer he looked straight at me "did you hear me? You said that the parcel was addressed to a Mr Black, but we know that's a lie!" leaning forward and drumming his fingers on the table, "we know that the parcel was addressed to you." He sat back in his chair without taking his eyes off of me.

"Well, yes it was." My mind is whirling "but the note inside said that I should ring Mr Black to arrange for him to come and collect it!"

"So how do you know Mr Black?" I really didn't like Brian Hurford as he was beginning to rile me "What is your involvement with the delivery of the parcel? How much are you paid for these deliveries?"

"Deliveries? Getting paid? What are you talking about?" If this was a bad dream then I wanted to wake up now. "I received one parcel from my friend Suzie asking me to phone Mr Black. There are no deliveries and no payment. Just one parcel with a dress for his wife." I didn't divulge the them what Mr Black had previously said about not knowing Suzie, or the fact that he didn't have a wife. "If you don't believe me look in my kitchen bin, I screwed the note up and tossed it in there."

The two detectives look at each other, suddenly Mak Wilson got up and walked over to the door, "you say that the note is in the kitchen bin?" I nodded. Opening the door, I heard him speak to someone, who must have been waiting outside in the corridor, "send someone back to the house, tell them to look for a note in the kitchen bin." With that he closed the door and walked back across the room to join his colleague and me at the table. "This Suzie, who is she?"

"She's just a friend, I've known her for years. She asked me to out and spend some time with her after my divorce." I shrugged "nothing sinister, she's just a friend!"

After a good few hours, they finally let me go home. It seems strange to me that they were interested in that parcel and had not mentioned anything about the London shop, but as they hadn't mentioned it, neither had I!

Chapter 15

As soon as I shut my front door the tears started to flow, not delicate little tears but huge sobs that racked my whole body. I fumbled my way blindly to the staircase and collapsed in a shaking sobbing heap on the bottom stair. The last time that I had sat here, was when I had phone Suzie to tell her that I was going to take her up on her offer to join her in Barbados, that was a joyful time, this was not!

I felt exhausted, everything seemed to be floating around me and I couldn't think straight. "I need a shower" I stated out loud "a shower and a decent cup of coffee!"

With the warm water rushing over my body the confusion of the previous hours seemed to start gelling in my brain. Talking out loud, usually helped me to clear any problems. "What the hell was that all about! Why were they being so cagy and wouldn't give me any real explanation. Surely if they knew about the delivery to my home, they would also have connected me to the London shop. Why had there been no mention of that? I couldn't believe that Suzie would send a 'special dress' to my home, please God let her confirm that she wouldn't? None of it made any sense."

After dressing I made up my mind to phone Suzie, I needed her to clarify who Mr Black was and that it was just an ordinary dress, although deep down I knew that it wasn't. Perhaps she could shed some light on how or why the police would raid my home and not the shop. As my hand reached out towards the phone I stopped myself from picking it up, a thought suddenly struck me what if they had bugged my phone! "What are you a spy or something?" but a nagging doubt stopped me from using the house phone. "A pay as you go phone is what I need" I clarified to myself "I'll go into town and buy one and then I'll phone Suzie from that." Satisfied that I had made the right decision I grabbed my bag and marched purposefully out of the door.

The morning had been trying to say the least, and the spotty young salesman in the phone shop had made me lose my temper by insisting that I really didn't want a pay as you go but needed a contract phone instead. After hearing raised voices, mostly mine, the store manager had intervened, and after what seemed like hours I walked out of the shop with the pay as you go phone, and a very sarcastic "Have a nice day!" from the spotty young salesman.

After finally assembling the phone and adding money to the account, which was trickier than I had expected, I once again sat on the bottom stair and dialled Suzie's number. After a while her answer phone cut in "Hi, this is Suzie. I'm either out getting drunk, getting laid or doing both. So, leave your message and I'll get back to you." The message normally made me smile, but somehow it didn't seem funny today. "Suzie, this is Polly ring me immediately that you pick up" quickly adding "only ring this number, do not ring the house phone or my mobile number. Suzie this is urgent!" with that I clicked the little phone shut.

The tinny sound of the phone ringing made me jump, "Polly, what's so bloody urgent that you can't let this old cougar sleep!" She sounded slightly drunk.

"My bloody house being invaded by hundreds of police and being dragged off to their stinking station and put in a cell, that's what so bloody URGENT!" I know that I slightly exaggerated the earlier event, but I felt the need to shock her. "All over that bloody parcel for Mr bloody Black!"

"POLICE!" she almost shouted down the phone. "What did you say? Had Mr Black already collected the parcel? What department were they?" she didn't sound drunk anymore, but she did sound in a complete panic.

"Yes, the bloody police and not just any department but he BLOODY DRUG SQUAD." This last bit I shouted down the phone. "What the hell was in that bloody parcel? Suzie, please tell me it wasn't drugs!"

"No, of course not." But her voice didn't sound convincing "Are there any 'special dresses' still waiting for collection at the shop? When I didn't answerer immediately "Polly, please focus. Are there any 'special dresses' at the shop?"

"No. Well there wasn't when I left yesterday, unless any have been delivered today. Do you want me to check with Marie?"

"No, it's okay Don's in London he can go over and check." She paused and then to my surprise added "Did they take your passport?"

"My passport? No of course not. Why do you ask?" My mind was in such a whirl that nothing made any sense anymore.

"Look, I'm sure that there's nothing to worry about, but just to be on the safe side I want you to come back here." I could hear her tapping on what I assumed was her laptop "there's a flight at 5.00 am tomorrow from Gatwick, North Terminal. I'll book the ticket from here and you can collect it at the airport." After a moments silence. "Polly, only bring hand luggage. I'll sort out everything you need at this end. Take care lovely." With that she was gone.

The following morning, as I walk into the airport my usual fears return. I think that every police officer and all of the security staff are watching me. A saying that my mother always used to mutter when my father would do the same thing over and over again, he had dementia, sprang into my head 'C'est reparti, or here we go again!'

Walking as steadily and as nonchalantly as I could manage, I make my way to the correct desk and calmly ask the heavily made-up assistant for my ticket. After a few clicks on her keyboard and after examining my passport she hands both the ticket and my passport to me. She confirms that my flight will be boarding in 20 minutes and advises me that I need to go straight to boarding gate 15. Once in the departure lounge I start to relax a little, and to my surprise when I eventually look at my ticket I see that Suzie has booked me into first class.

My mind sweeps back to flights taken with Steve, when he would not so quietly berate the people who turned left whilst we always turned right.

"I suppose that they think that they're something special." He would mutter as he squashed into the cramped seats of economy. *"Don't they realise that most people on this plane could afford to sit up there!"* At this he would incline his head to the front of the plane, *"but most of us are more sensible than to waste good money for a bit more space!"*

I wondered if when she stole my husband if she gad grand ideas of shopping sprees and luxury holidays. He might have a successful company but he's still a skinflint or at least he was for the duration of our marriage.

I for one was glad that I had space to relax. Taking the headphones out of their little pouch, I switched around several channels until I found some lovely soft music. Once the meal had been served and I had savoured a very good glass of wine, I settled down to get some sleep. My mind was still all over the place, and I woke with a start. Hearing a noise to my left I looked across the aisle and into the soft brown eyes of a man. "That must have been some dream. I wasn't sure if you were enjoying it or not!" His eyes seemed to dance as he spoke.

Straightening myself up, as best I could, "Oh dear, I'm sorry if I disturbed you. That glass of wine seems to have gone to my head."

Holding out his hand in my direction he introduced himself "I'm Joe."

Although I really didn't want to be bothered with small talk, I also didn't want to be rude, "Hi, I'm Polly."

"Are you holidaying or on business?" when I didn't answer immediately he continued "Sorry don't mean to be nosy, it's my job!"

"No, it's okay. I'm visiting a friend." I didn't mention Suzie but let him think that it might be a man. As nice as he seemed I didn't want to be bothered with anyone.

"Lucky you, I'm on business." He still didn't mention what his business was and to be honest I wasn't really interested. I was glad when he leaned his head back and shut his eyes. Something about him disturbed me, but I couldn't put my finger on what it was.

As the plane's seat belt light clicked off, I stood and reached up to collect my bag from the overhead locker, losing my balance I bumped into Joe, who was also pulling his luggage from the opposite locker, "Sorry" was all that I could say, as I turned to be met with those amazing eyes.

"Is your friend coming to meet you? I'm hiring a car, so if you need a lift anywhere!" I noticed that as he spoke he raised an eyebrow.

"I'm not sure, but if my friend can't come, I'm sure that someone will have been sent to collect me." As I spoke I realised how grand that must have sounded.

As we left the aircraft I was thrilled to see Jonathon standing to the right of the planes steps, and parked behind him was the big white SUV. I heard a low whistle from behind me and then Joe's voice whisper "Well, we must have a VIP on board, wonder who it is?"

As I reach the ground Jonathon rushed forward to take my hand luggage. I turn and give Joe the sweetest of smiles before climbing into the waiting vehicle.

On the journey to Suzie's, Jonathon informed me that Don had been to the shop and had confirmed that it was all clear. Apparently Suzie had to go over to St Lucia on business and had told Jonathon to take me to her home and that she would see me in the morning. Looking at the clock on the car's dashboard I saw that it was 9.00 pm.

I was glad when we eventually arrived at Suzie's as my muscles were starting to complain, how I wished that Suzie had a bathtub at her home instead of just showers. I would really have liked to have a nice long luxurious soak. Later standing in the shower with the hot water washing over me, a sudden realisation struck me, did this now mean that I could never go home!

I had confirmed with Margaret, who stayed at the house, for a good portion of the week whilst I was in London, that she could look after the house for me for the foreseeable future. I hated lying to her, but for whatever reason I didn't want her to know that I had returned to Barbados. It would be good to have someone moving around inside the house, if someone was watching the place, then they would see lights going on and off which might make them think that it was me.

It was after 10.00 am the following morning when I finally woke up, blearily I headed for the kitchen. My stomach was growling as I hadn't eaten since the meal on the plane. I had just opened the fridge door to see what I could eat, when I heard a key in the front door lock. Silently I prayed it was Suzie!

"Thank god you're here!" she flew across the space that separated us and hugged me tightly, "I need to know all about it" holding me away from her "you look dreadful, did you manage to sleep?"

"I'm fine, just ravenous." I turn back to the fridge "looks like bacon and eggs. Do you want some?" That morning even the finest caviar wouldn't have tasted any better that my meal of bacon and eggs.

Suzie picks up the coffee peculator that is bubbling away and pours us both a mug of strong coffee. "I really need to know what happened with the police, Polly." She hands me that steaming mug of coffee "was it just the parcel that they were interested in?"

"That's all they asked me about" after eating some of my breakfast and taking a gulp of my coffee, I was starting to feel a little bit more civilised "not one mention of the shop!"

Suzie thought for a moment "Did you notice if anyone followed you from the airport?"

"I don't think so. But ….." hesitating for a split second my mind went back to Joe "no, I'm sure it's nothing!"

"What? Did something happen?" Suzie's voice sounds quite shrill.

"There was a man on the plane, he seemed quite interested in why I was coming to Barbados." Scratching my head I continued "He kept saying that he was coming here on business, but never said what his business was."

"What was his name? Did he give you his card?" Now Suzie sounded quite rattled.

"He just introduced himself to me as Joe." Suzie looked uncomfortable "but the strange thing was that we had only spoken half a dozen words and he asked me if I needed a lift somewhere. Thinking about it now, he did seem to be prying." I stopped before adding "or maybe he was just being friendly!"

Chapter 16

I had been staying with Suzie for just over a month, when all hell seemed to break loose.

"Polly, Polly for Christ's sake wake up!" blearily I opened my eyes to see Suzie ashen faced sitting on the edge of the bed cradling the house phone in her lap "it's Margaret." She pushed the phone into my hand.

"Margaret?" I stifled a yawn and pushed myself up to a sitting position.

"For god's sake Polly speak to her!" Suzie sounded really frantic.

I pressed the speaker button "Margaret, hello is everything alright?" Suzie let out a laugh and muttered something under her breath "Margaret are you still there?"

"The police have been here this afternoon looking for you," I could hear the tremble in my friends voice "Polly you didn't tell me that you were going to Barbados, why didn't you tell me?" before I could answer she went on "I told them that you were at the shop in London. When they left I rang the shop to tell you that they wanted to speak to you, and it was then that Marie told me that you had gone abroad. What do they want to speak to about? Do you know?" I could hear how upset she was, and I felt awful for lying to her.

"I'm sorry that I didn't tell you. It was all a bit of a rush." I looked over at Suzie who was now pacing back and forth by the bedroom window. "Did they give you a name or number for me to contact?"

"Yes, he said his was Detective Chief Inspector Mark Wilson. He said that already had his number. Why do you have his number? Polly what is going on?" her voice now had a frightened edge to it, "I don't think that I want to stay her anymore, I don't feel safe. When are you coming back?"

"I'm not sure" again I look at Suzie for some inspiration, but none is given, "if you don't want to stay at the house, just lock it up and go home." I realised how hard that must have sounded at the other end of the line, so I quickly add "I'm sorry that you have been put through this. I am really grateful for everything that you have done, but I don't want you to feel uncomfortable."

"I will go home for a few days, will you let me know when you're back?" her voice sounded hollow as it echoed down the line.

"Yes of course, Margaret please don't worry I'll sort everything out." As soon as I had spoken she was gone.

I was just about to hand the phone back to Suzie when it rang again. Suzie ran across the room and snatched it out of my hand "Hello…..Yes, this is Suzie….. Yes, she's here, just a moment." From the look on her face, I knew that this was going to be more bad news. "It's Marie."

"Hi Marie" I tried to sound as calm as possible, which was difficult with Suzie pacing and muttering at the side of the bed.

Without any pleasantries Marie's voice crackled down the line "The shops been raided!"

"Oh Christ. Is everyone alright?" I leaned my head back against the pillows to stop the room from spinning.

"Bugger, is everyone alright, were there any special dresses on the premises?" Suzie shouted at me "ask her if they found anything?"

"I heard" Marie sounded angry "Tell that ungrateful bitch that no, there was nothing for them to find and yes, Polly, everyone here is fine, a bit shaken but other than that alright." She paused "thank you for asking."

"What reason did they give for the raid? Did they interview anyone?" My rational brain was starting to work.

"They said that they had information that we had drugs on the premises." Her voice now seemed a little calmer "As luck would have it we were just about to close for the day, so it was only me and Jemma left in the shop when the police burst in" I heard a cup being placed back on a saucer as she continued "they asked about the dresses and who supplied them. They seemed surprised when I told them that our supplier was based in the Caribbean." Again, the clink of crockery "They have taken the order book away. I asked them if we can still trade, and they have confirmed that we can."

For the second time in less than an hour, I found myself apologizing "I am so sorry that you and Jemma have been put through this. If you don't feel like opening the shop then don't. Why don't you take a few days off?" I didn't look at Suzie as I added "On full pay of course."

"Thank you Polly, I think that's a good idea. Will we see you soon?" I was glad that her voice sounded a lot calmer.

"I hope so, now go home and rest." With that she was gone.

"Fuck, fuck, fuck." Suzie was slumped in the chair that stood next to the window. "This couldn't have happened at a worse time!" she rubbed her hands over her face, "Jose arrives today, he is not going to be pleased."

"Jose! Who the hell is Jose?" I spat the words out. "Forget about this bloody Jose character, shouldn't you be more worried about Margaret and the others who have, through no fault of their own, been put through the wringer!"

"Forget about Jose! Are you bloody kidding? If he's heard about all of this, then what they've been through will nothing that the rest of us will have to endure!" I could tell from her eyes that she was absolutely petrified.

Getting out of bed, I walked over to where she was sitting hunched over in the chair, taking her hand I gently stated, "I think that you had better tell me who he is and what he has to do with the business."

With wide frightened eyes she explained, "Jose Escodracon, is the head of the Columbus Cartel. He is arriving today to celebrate our success." At this she gave a sick little laugh "We are supposed to be throwing a party on Tobias's yacht tonight." I notice that her body is shaking, "bloody hell Polly, what are we going to do?"

"Well, we could play it cool and hope that he hasn't heard about it," I stood up to stretch my legs "Where's Don? Perhaps he'll know how to play it!" A sudden thought struck me, "Anway, what does this Jose do? How can we possibly be to blame about events in London, when we're here!"

Suzie tilted her head to one side, as if she was thinking about something before she too had a lightbulb moment, "Polly, you're a bloody genius." Suzie gave a small smile, "As you say how can anyone here be held responsible or made to take the blame?"

"Now, what's all this about a party, am I supposed to be going to it and if so I hope that you have got a decent dress for me to wear." I tried to keep my voice as light as possible, whilst my stomach was tying itself in knots. That same old feeling was starting to bubble away in my gut!

Suzie spent the rest of the day either on the phone or pacing the floor, which in the end made me feel so uneasy that I cried off of the party. "I don't think that I want to attend this party this evening, my head is all over the place and I don't think that I will be very good company."

"Oh no, you have to be there Jose wants to meet you." She walked over to the drinks cabinet and poured two large glasses of rum "he likes to eyeball anyone involved in his business."

"Excuse me, his business? What are you talking about?" I except the glass that she was offering me, placing it on the table next to my chair, "I thought that this was your business?"

"Well, yes it is, but he's my main supplier" she took a slug of her drink "to be honest he's my only supplier!"

Later that evening Jonathon pulled up outside Suzie's in the stretch limousine and as we walked out onto the porch I asked "Are the girls in there? Nodding my head towards the vehicle, when Suzie didn't answer "Oh, no for a moment I thought that this was going to be a classy dinner, as you hold this man in such high regard. But here we go again for another knocking shop night of pleasure!"

Suzie grabbed my arm, "Don't go on the boat with that sort of attitude, he won't like it." Lowering her voice, "The girls are coming as a distraction for his boys, he doesn't like them around when he is talking business." With that she walked away and got into the car.

Chapter 17

As I step out of the car onto the dockside, my stomach is again doing somersaults as a bad feeling takes over the whole of my body and I genuinely feel sick. As I stand there looking up at the yacht, I can hear Suzie, who is still in the car, issuing instructions to the girls.

The girls eventually emerge from the car and wiggle their way up the gang plank towards to burly men who have been watching us since our arrival. They are obviously guarding the entrance to the yacht. As the girls step onto the deck the men say something to them and they immediately raise their arms in the air. One by one the men frisk them, and then run a metal detector over each girls body, only when the men are completely satisfied are they allowed to pass.

Suzie takes me arm as we walk towards the yacht, "Remember what I said Polly no attitude!" She steps in front of me and as we near the men she automatically raises her arms, I follow suit.

The girls head off through the door to the salon and I guess that Jose's men are waiting in there to be entertained, as a loud cheer goes up as the girls make their entrance.

A raspy voice with a very thick accent, emanates from our left although I can't be sure I would think that the owner is either Mexican or South American, for some reason the voice makes my flesh crawl!

"At last, we meet." I turn in the direction of the voice and to my amazement I see a wizened little man, who can't be more than five feet tall, he has greasy long dark hair pulled back into a ponytail, that falls halfway down his back. I desperately try not to smile at his attire, as he has a white shirt open to his navel with the biggest gold medallion draped around his neck. His spindly little legs are encased in tight black leather trousers and the whole ensemble is finished off by a pair of highly decorated boots, that I notice have quite a high Cuban heel. His face is the colour and texture of dried leather. The most striking thing about him is his eyes, they are a vibrant green and narrow as a snakes.

"Turn around" I do as he orders and as I came back to face him a shudder runs through the whole of my body, "Not bad, for an old broad. I take it Suzie has filled you in and you understand what tonight is all about."

I'm about to answer, when Suzie quickly speaks "It's okay Jose, she's completely up to date." She shoots a look in my direction, "No problems here! Now do I spy chilled champagne?" She nudges me to start walking "Shall we enjoy a glass with our dinner?"

Jose turns on his Cuban heels, and with a click of his fingers a man jumps forward and pours the champagne, "How many girls have you brought?" as he speaks he licks his lips "I hope that they are good!" With that he rubs the front of his trousers and sneering continues, "my boys haven't been home for a long time, so they are looking forward to a very good time." Moving closer to Suzie "they better not be disappointed!" Suzie confirms that her girls are the best and then no-one will be left unsatisfied "Good now where is Don, he should be here?"

"I don't know as I haven't spoken to him today." As she speaks she glances at her watch "would you like me to call him?"

"No" I have to try very hard not to cringe as he looks me up and down "it might be better if he's not here, I have some things to discuss with the two of you lovely ladies and he might get in the way." Turning away he waves his hand towards the upper deck and the engines start up.

"I really think that we should wait for Don." I say more to Suzie than anyone else, "after all he is part of the business." Suzie doesn't answer but I can tell from her eyes that she is now very worried. I know that I would feel a lot safer with Don on board and I get the distinct impression that so would Suzie.

Before long the dock is a blip on the horizon and any hope of Don joining us has quickly disappeared. As we walk through to the dining room Suzie whispers "Whatever happens stay with me!" from the way that she squeezes my hand I know that she also feels that this is not a good situation.

We take our places at the table and I notice that a fourth place has been set, and I assume that the table was laid in anticipation of Don being on the yacht. Suddenly I notice that Suzie goes very pale and is staring past me to the deck area, as I turn to follow the line of her eyes I see the biggest man that I have ever seen lumbering towards us. He must be at least 6 foot 7 and weigh a breath taking 600 lbs. Without a word he joins us at the dining table and Jose indicates to the male servant to serve the dinner.

The dinner itself is remarkable, lobster tails with caviar and finely cooked vegetables all served on the finest bone china and although it looks and smells delicious I don't have an appetite. Surprisingly most of the conversation is pleasant. Jose asks me about my family and I tell him that I really don't have any now that both my mum and dad have past. He tuts at this and says that he would be lost without his wife and 10 children. The other man doesn't utter a word, but just sits and eats.

At the end of the meal Jose suggest that we take a brandy and sit outside to enjoy the evening air. Once we are all seated he turns to his companion and with a sneer says, "Well my friend, why don't you tell these lovely ladies why you have joined us tonight." Without moving his head, he looks at us from the corner of his eye, for a moment he reminded again of a snake which was about to strike. "I'm sure that they are anxious to know!" he leans closer to the other man and mutters "Por favour cuenteles sobre neuestro problema, mi amigo."

The big man leans back further against the cream leather cushions of the sofa and takes a long draw on his big fat cigar. Narrowing his eyes he looks straight at the two of us, "I've had some news from London" I feel Suzie tense on the seat next to me, "I'm told that there have been some raids, now it puzzles me whey neither of you…." Stopping to take another long drag on his cigar "or come to that Don thought that it wasn't important enough to mention it to us." Suzie started to speak "Shut up, I haven't finished speaking, "his voice was unusually high for such a big man, "first I'm told that a few weeks ago your house was raided" he points his fat cigar at me "and that you were questioned by the filth at the police station and then only yesterday the coppers were back at your house again, closely followed by the London shop raid," his dark eyes seemed to glint in the moonlight "So how much does your friend Margaret know?"

"Margaret?" I couldn't stop the tremble in my voice "Margaret didn't even know that I was out of the country!"

"So how did she know to send them to the shop?" Jose leaned forward in his seat as he spoke.

"She thought that I was in London and assumed that if they wanted to talk to me that I would be there." I didn't like the tone of this conversation at all and tried to calm the atmosphere down, "I'm sure that all of it is a case of mistaken identity, after all what would the drug squad want with either me or the shop!"

"Is she a bloody idiot or what?" Jose addressed this question to Suzie, "what does she mean, what do the drug squad want!" jumping to his feet he shouted at me "the bloody drug drugs you moron, that's what!" with that he slapped me so hard across the face that I went flying across the leather cushions and fell at the big man's feet with a thump.

Shaking my head to try and clear my thoughts I looked up at him from my crumpled position on the deck boards "Drugs? What drugs?" I looked across at Suzie who was now quivering with fear "you didn't tell me about any drugs, you told me gold, liquid gold!" when she didn't answer I pleaded with her "Suzie, you told me gold, please tell them that I know nothing about any drugs!"

Both the big man and Jose were now looking from me to Suzie and back again in total confusion, until suddenly the big man let out a huge belly laugh, "Oh, I see, you told your friend gold so that she would join you. If you had told her drugs you knew that she would say no, am I right?" With that he prodded me with one of his huge feet, when I didn't answer he gave me a swift kick in the ribs, "did you hear me? What sort of an idiot are you? Did you really think that we would set up this whole organisation just to smuggle gold!" with that both men laughed "Christ, you really are stupid!"

"So are we to believe that neither of you or any of your helpers in London have blabbed to the filth," Jose bent down level with my head, I was still winded from the kick in the ribs and found that I could only nod my head in reply. "Unfortunately for you we can't let you go back to London if they're still interested in you." He looked to where the other man was still sitting and menacingly added "Can we?" Straightening up he ordered me to my feet. Once I was standing and without taking his eyes off of me he continued "take off your dress." When I didn't do it immediately, he took a step towards me "take it off or he will take it off for you." With that he indicated the other man. My hands were trembling so much that I found it hard to unzip my beautiful dress, but at last the zip moved and the dress fell to the ground. Jose looked me up and down and turning to the big man stated, "such a nice body, such a waste!"

I heard a gasp from Suzie, "Jose, please she hasn't said anything to anyone." Her eyes were darting wildly between the two men "I can vouch for her; she really did think that it was liquid gold and not coke. I knew if she knew the truth that she would have nothing to do with it. Please Jose, please don't do this!"

In what seemed like one movement he grabbed Suzie's arm and pulled her to her feet, "Someone has to pay for my lost revenue, maybe you'd like to take your friends place." His eyes seemed to bore right into her soul, "With your silence I take it that's a no." Swinging her round by the arm he growled "Get in there" as he pushed her towards the salon door "and stay in there until I tell you to come out!" Without looking at me she did as she was told, leaving me alone, trembling with fear on the deck in just my bra and knickers, not knowing or understanding what these two maniacs had in store for me.

Once Suzie was out of sight Jose, without taking his eyes off me, took my face in his hands and in a soft voice mutter "Cuanto antes esto termine, mejor."

As soon as the words were spoken the big man slowly got up form his seat, as he stood up he threw the rest of his cigar over the side of the yacht and into the sea. Before I could move he had lifted me off of my feet and with my face so close to his, that I could smell the cigar smoke on his breath, he swung me up into his arms as he flatly said, "Time to feed the fishes." With that he dropped me over the side of the yacht and into the cold dark water below.

Chapter 18

The coldness of the water took my breath away. I felt myself sinking down through the dark water and into its murky underworld. The water seemed to be sucking me down into its hidden belly as if it was ready to consume me. I honestly thought that I was about to die, but my survival instinct suddenly kicked in and I fought my way back up to the surface.

As I struggled for breath, I watch as the lights on the yacht move further and further away. Even in my panicked state of mind I was sure that any minute Tobias would swing the yacht around and they would come back and fish me out of the sea, having taught me a lesson, how wrong was I.

As the hours slip away my limbs, from numbness brought on by the cold water and fatigue from treading water, start to feel heavy and I could feel myself gradually slipping into unconsciousness. Remembering my swimming lessons from years ago, I decide to float on my back to give my body a break and I start to quietly sing to myself so that I wouldn't fall asleep. I knew that if I slept that would mean certain death.

The sounds of the sea at night will always haunt me, random splashing noises seem to be magnified in the quiet of the night. Suddenly something big seemed to be diving in and out of the water not far from where I am lying, trying to keep as still as possible I tried to work out exactly where the sound was coming from. A thought suddenly makes me stiff with fear and I send a quiet prayer up to heaven "please god don't let it be a shark, I don't want to end my life in the belly of a shark!!" In the back of my mind, I am sure that I have read somewhere that it is very rare to find sharks in the Caribbean, but knowing my luck tonight this would be one of those rare occasions.

My only hope is that Suzie is safely back on shore and that she will alert someone, maybe Don, and I will be rescued. I have to make sure that I get through tonight talking out loud to myself seems to help, so I start to not only sing but also recite any poem that I can remember. Ironically I remember every verse of the 'Old Man of the Sea' a poem that my grandfather used to tell me. Thinking about it now I realise that it was actually more of a sea shanty than a poem. But floating in the middle of nowhere I guess that it doesn't really matter what it is, reciting it is keeping me awake.

At last, the sky begins to get light, I have no idea how long I have been alone floating and drifting in and out of sleep. I look around hoping that I may see land, but all I see is the vast expanse of the ocean.

I don't understand how Suzie could have just left me here. However, frightened she was she is, surely she must be able to find a way to get someone to come back and rescue me. Something triggers in my brain I'm assuming that she made it back to shore, but how do I know that she isn't out there floating in the dark water like me. Frantically I start to scan the surface of the ocean for as far as I can see, but there is nothing, no land, and no Suzie and more importantly no boats.

My lips and mouth are so dry that I can literally feel my lips crack when I try to speak out loud. The sun is beginning to rise and I know that before long the temperature will be unbearable. The heat will only make my salt-soaked skin dryer and I am terrified that it will crack and bleed, alerting any passing shark to my presence.

I must have slipped into sleep as when I open my eyes the sun is high in the sky and I gauge that it must be around noon. A little voice deep in my brain starts talking to me, "Why prolong the inevitable, you're going to die, so just get it over with. No-one is coming. They all think that your dead anyway. The papers will say 'Middle-aged British woman lost at sea after a night of drunken debauchery on a friends yacht'. I imagine who will be at my funeral, Margaret will be distraught and Steve, well he'll most probably celebrate. I don't suppose that Suzie will be there.

Just as I am seriously contemplating diving down into the deep blue sea a noise arouses me from my despair. At first I can't make out what it is but suddenly realisation kicks in, it's a helicopter flying low over the ocean. A sudden surge of energy fills my body and I frantically wave, I don't shout as I know that over the noise of the engine that they won't hear me. To my horror the helicopter flies right over me and continues on into the distance. Tears of despair flow down over my salt cracked cheeks, as I watch the helicopter disappear towards the horizon.

"Well, that's it" the nagging little voice starts up again "they won't search this area again, it will have been given an all-clear code. Face it you're all on your own."

"God, if you want me to die then make it quick." I shout up at the sky above "I'm just going to lie here in this bloody ocean and you can come and do your worst. Just bloody get on with it!"

As the daylight starts to fade, I know that I cannot survive another night. I'm starting to see things, today I found myself trying to swim to what I thought was a little island only to look again and it was gone. Dehydration is setting in and I know that I won't last much longer. Scanning the horizon, I see a boat which seems to be heading towards me. "For Christ sake God do you really have to play these tricks on me, just let me die." I close my eyes and feel myself drift into sleep, silently praying that this will be the end.

Suddenly I feel something tucking at my arms and a voice calling my name, for a minute I think that God as answered my prayers and that an angel has come down to take, me to my eternal resting place. But wait, I hear a number of voices and someone's hands are firmly under my armpits hauling me upwards.

"Polly, Polly can you open your eyes?" A male voice sounds very close to my ear. Slowly I open my eyes, but my sight is blurry and I can't make out who it is. The same voice now sounds quite triumphant "She's alive, thank the lord she's alive." As my sight starts to clear I look straight into the worried eyes of Don.

Chapter 19

I awoke with a fright, looking around the room I couldn't place where I am. It certainly wasn't Suzie's. This room was all white and chrome not all like Suzie's colourful house, this place is far too plain with no colour anywhere. I can't get my bearings. The last thing that I remember was seeing Don, so where is he now? Everything feels really strange, is it me or is the room moving! I can hear what sounds like a distant hum, maybe an engine in the distance.

Lying there I start to panic, maybe the movement is the sea and I'm back on the boat. What awful thing do they plan to do to me now! Again, for the umpteenth time, since being thrown in the sea, I pray "Dear God, please don't let me back on that boat. Please don't let them hurt me again."

As I try to move my body screams out, the pain is unbearable. My skin is so sore and taut from being in the sea for so long, that just trying to move is torture. Slowly I try to move my arm and as I do I notice a tube that is attached to a needle in my arm. A clear liquid is gently dripping from a bag, that is held high up on a metal stand and I can see the clear liquid running down inside the tube towards the needle in my arm. What if they are trying to poison me, they couldn't drown me, so now they are going for a sure-fire way to finish me off. Just as I am trying to summon up the strength to remove the needle, the door opens and in walks Don, "Glad to see that you're awake at last." For some reason, the sound of his voice makes me feel safe.

"Where am I?" my voice comes out in a squeak as my throat is so sore and I try to swallow, tears of pain start running from my eyes as I manage to croak, "Don, am I safe?"

Walking across the room he pulls a chair up to the side of the bed and gently takes my hand, he quietly says "Yes" he seems to find it difficult to look at me and with his eyes firmly fixed on the bedsheet he says "Polly, I am so sorry for what has happened to you, we had no idea that they would go so far."

"We" you said we. Do you mean you and Suzie? Where is she?" My questions came out in a strange little voice.

"No, not Suzie and me!" At last, he raised his eyes to meet mine, "Polly, I work or should I say worked undercover for the drug squad, back in the UK." He paused as if waiting from me to say something and when I don't he continues "for the last couple of years I have been working to try to bring down the Columbus Cartel, which as you now know is run by Jose Escodracon and Pablo Cortenda. It was their plan to infiltrate the UKs drug market to see if the 'special dresses' would get past customs, if they did then they were planning to take America by storm."

"But what about Suzie?" as I ask I lie my head back against the pillows, my eyes feel heavy and I want to sleep "I feel like I am having a bad dream and that soon I will wake up and none of this will be true. I'm finding it hard to understand. All of this is too much to take in!"

On hearing this Don stood "I think that the rest of the explanation should wait until you are feeling stronger."

As he was about to close the door I asked "Don, why does it feel like the room is moving?"

For the first time for a long time, I heard that throaty Scottish laugh "The room isn't moving, but the plane is!" at that moment my eyes closed and I drift off to sleep.

Something is tugging at me pulling me this way and that "Shark, shark!" I scream as I start to struggle, flailing my arms and kicking my legs.

"Stop, Polly stop" opening my eyes I see a youngish woman standing at my bedside "I'm sorry but I have to fasten you in, we're going in to be landing in about 10 minutes."

Frowning as she pulls at straps that are crossed over my body "Please lie still."

"Landing? Where are we landing?" I cannot keep the fear out of my voice, "are you taking me back to Barbados?"

"No, of course not." She turns away from me and starts towards the door.

"Please tell me where we are?" I feel very vulnerable strapped into this bed with my head being the only part of me that I can move.

"England!" she snaps the word out "and with any luck straight to prison for you." Checking that no-one is outside the door she struts back across the room and leaning over me with her face only inches from mine she snarls "My brother died from a drugs overdose and if I had my way all of you drug traffickers would rot in jail.!"

"Well, it's a good job that it's not up to you then isn't it PC Noble!" A deep Scottish baritone booms from the doorway, "Get out. If you know what's good for you you'll stay well away from Polly and me." Don held the door open but as she approached him he stated "As soon as we land report to the airport police, do you understand? I don't think that you belong on this case." As she didn't answer he repeated "PC Noble, do you understand?" She curtly nodded her head and disappeared out of the door, "are you okay?" I confirmed that I was "Good. We will be landing at Gatwick soon, so I need to go and buckle up. I'll see you soon after we land."

As I lie here strapped in and helpless, the events of the last two days keep swimming around in my head. I still don't understand how anyone could do that to another human being, just throw them in the sea and let them drown. How do these people sleep at night? I thought about Suzie and after all of the years that we have known each other, why would she get me involved in this awful situation. I wondered why Don hadn't mentioned her. Was he hiding something, perhaps she had been thrown overboard and he didn't want to tell me that she hadn't survived. All of these awful thoughts kept coming and going. I could still smell the cigar smoke on the man's breath, who I now know to be Pablo Cortenda. Nothing seems real, I feel like I'm watching some dreadful Hollywood movie.

"Oh, dear God" Said that little nagging voice in my head "that awful woman said prison!" lying there I tried to think about cases of drugs couriers that I had read about in the national press, but my mind couldn't focus and as the plane started it's decent the nagging little voice whispered, "You'll be an old and grey by the time you're free." With that thought ringing in my head I start to weep.

Chapter 20

As the plane touches down Don and another man, who I feel I should recognise come into the room, "You are going to be taken straight to hospital." Don started to release the bed from the floor straps that had been holding it in place, "due to the nature of your illness we have told the hospital that you have been involved in a nasty boating accident out in the channel. From now on you will be known as Christina Burton, do you understand?"

"No, not really." I noticed the look that passed between the two men, was it frustration or anger, I really couldn't tell.

"Polly! We cannot let anyone know that you are in fact still alive. If the cartel know that they were unsuccessful we are sure that they will send someone to finish the job!" As Don spoke a shiver shook my whole body. "We have secured a private hospital room and our plain clothes officers will act as family members and friends. We are unable to post an armed guard outside of the door as this, obviously, would arouse suspicion, but someone will be with you at all times."

As Don and his colleague wheeled me towards the open aeroplane door, I was surprised to see that we were parked far away from the terminal, in a spot near a huge warehouse. As soon as we came into sight two paramedics rushed forward and skilfully manhandled me off the bed and onto a stretcher, which they used to take me down the plane's steps and into the waiting ambulance.

Whilst the paramedics gave me a quick check and secured that bag containing the clear liquid up on a hook, that was situated near the roof of the ambulance, I could hear Don and the other man talking in low voices. I was relieved when Don climbed into the back of the vehicle and travelled with me to the hospital.

The journey took over an hour and by the time we reached our destination I had got used to being called Christina. Don had peppered his conversation with the name so many times that I now answered without hesitation. As soon as the ambulance arrived I was whisked straight up to the private wing and into my room.

Don had stopped at the reception desk to speak with the on-duty sister, asking her to issue instructions to her staff that I was not to be unnecessarily disturbed. He informed her that a family member would be staying with me at all times and would be able to take care of all of my needs. From the bit of conversation that I could hear I don't think that the sister was very happy about it and I heard her say "Well, I think that we had better see what Matron has to say about all of this." To which I heard Don curtly reply "Tell Matron to speak to Mr Zehan, who is, as I am sure that you know, an esteemed consultant. I'm sure that he will want Mrs Burton, who is a private patient of his, wishes complied with. He will confirm that she is to be given the utmost respect and privacy."

As he walks away and into the room he mutters as he closes the door "Bloody jobsworth!"

I have now been in hospital a week and I am starting to feel a lot better. My 'family' members have strangely consisted of my first 'niece' who happens to be a nurse and every day she has been tending to the sores and sunburn on my body. My second 'niece' is a very accomplished hairdresser and has coloured my mousy hair to a deep auburn. Whilst my third 'niece', has brought me clothes, as the only thing that I had when I was rescued was my bra and knickers, both of which had quickly been removed and kept as evidence, being replace by a not very complimentary white jumpsuit. My 'nephews' have brought me books me books and food and have kept my entertained with board games and one has taught me how to play poker. It would have been lovely to meet all of these people under different circumstances.

On the second Monday of my hospital stay Don walks into the room, one glance at this face tells me that he's not happy. "Time to go Christina."

A feeling of dread starts to creep through my body "Go! Go where?" I look up at him from my seat next to the window "are you taking me to prison?"

Slowly he walks around the bed and perching on the edge he takes my hand in his "Not exactly" he keeps his eyes firmly on the ground.

"Don! Look at me. Where are you taking me?" I pull my hand away from him so quickly that he is forced to look at me as I repeat "Where are you taking me?"

"We need to move you to a safe house. You can't stay here any longer, people are starting to get suspicious." He nods his head towards the door. "That nosy bloody sister has been . comments about how funny it is that there has been no mention of a boating accident on the news." Standing he straightens his tie "so it's been decided that for your safety we are moving you to another location."

One of my 'nieces' is already waiting outside of the hospital room with a wheelchair. As soon as we walk out into the corridor I am told to sit in the chair and a thick heavy blanket is wrapped around me. When we walk through the heavy doors that act as a barrier, closing off the corridor that accommodates the private rooms, I see that one of my 'nephews' is standing next to an open lift door, which I notice he has jammed open with his foot. As soon as the lift reaches the ground floor, I am rushed into a waiting car and whisked away from the hospital grounds.

As we drive through London I watch the people rushing here and there without, what seems to me, a care in the world. I think back to how happy I was pottering around my lovely garden and enjoying the odd visit to the theatre which all seems like a lifetime ago. My eyes wander back to the unfolding scene outside and I wish with all of my heart that I was back in Somerset in my beloved garden.

The car suddenly takes a sharp right and I notice that we are heading out of London towards the Midlands. The journey seems to take forever and as the light begins to fade the lights of the cars coming towards us seem to be hypnotic and my eyes start to close.

I wake to Don calling me "Christina, wake up." As I open my eyes he climbs out of the car "here we are, home sweet home."

The house itself is nice, but it certainly isn't home! The perimeter is guarded by a row of very tall thick bushes and the little garden has not been loved for a very long time. The inside of the house is clean, but old, with creaking floorboards and windows that rattle in the wind. Still if it's safe then I suppose that's all that counts.

"I thought a nice fish and chip supper washed down with a decent red." Don hands Tom, the driver, some money "I saw what looked like a decent chippy just down the road, can you pop back and get us all some" as Tom went to leave the room, Don added "and don't forget the red" the younger man made a salute. After we had heard the front door close, Don looked at me "Are you really alright?"

"Well, now that you mention it there are some things that I would like to know," I sat down opposite him at the big wooden table, which took up most of the small kitchen space, "For instance, where is Suzie? Do you know what happened to her?"

After a moment he flatly stated "She's in jail! All of them are in jail." He tapped his fingers on the tabletop "When they arrived back in port, we were waiting for them. It's a very rare event that both Jose and Pablo are ever seen together, so along with our Caribbean counterparts we set up a sting to catch them before they had a chance to disappear again."

"Suzie, did Suzie tell you where to find me?" I couldn't look at him.

"I'm sorry to say that she didn't. In fact, as we rounded everyone up and asked if there was anyone else on the yacht it was Honey who asked where you were." He let out a long sigh "if it hadn't been for her we wouldn't have known that you had even been out on the boat that evening."

I was speechless, I couldn't believe that Suzie would have just abandoned me, when she had the opportunity to tell someone where I was. After a while I managed to compose myself "What's happened to the girls? Are they also in jail?"

Don shook his head "No, they did nothing wrong. After being questioned they were allowed to go" looking across the table at me he continued "it's strange but whatever you think about the girls lifestyles, Honey was the one that was most worried about you." He reached into his pocket and took out a silver chain with a small silver spider on it, which he handed to me "talking about Honey, I had forgotten that she gave this to me and asked that if we found you would I give it to you."

My emotions took over and I was unable to stop my tears from flowing "I remember her wearing this." Opening the catch, I secured it around my neck, my fingers gently caressed the little spider.si'

"In the Caribbean it's supposed to bring you luck if you see a white spider, I think that's why most of the spider charms are in sliver." Don informed me "If I remember rightly it's called 'Anansi' in old folklore."

I started to laugh, just a gentle chuckle that quickly escalated into a near hysterical full-blown gut-wrenching howl. The more I looked at Don's startled face the harder I laughed. It felt so good to at last rid myself of the pent-up emotions that I had been holding in over the last few weeks. The little spider danced at my throat, with every roar that left my mouth.

Don quickly got up and raced around the table to where I was sitting, cradling me in his arms he gently stroked my hair as he promised "Once you are completely better I will explain everything to you, but I don't think that now is a good time." I felt like a child in his arms "Take a few days to settle in here and then I promise we will talk!" As if on cue we heard Tom's key being pushed into the front door lock "Go and wash your face, once you've had something to eat and a good nights sleep you'll feel a lot better." Gently he pulled me to my feet and I did as I was told.

Chapter 21

Over the next few days, I settled into the new house, the creaks and groans of the old floorboards became a familiar sound and no longer a scary noise. As the weather was fine, I felt stir crazy staying in the house all day so I decided to try and tidy the garden.

The old garden shed, which stood at the end of the garden, held a treasure trove of old tools and after rummaging around I managed to find everything that I needed. I was so engrossed in trimming and dead heading the various rose bushes that I didn't hear Don approaching, his booming voice startled me so much that I almost fell into the neatly trimmed rose bed "Christina, what the hell are you doing? He sounded angry "I've told you not to come out here on your own! What would you have done if I had wanted to hurt you?" with that he hauled me to my feet "you must listen to what you are told!"

Suddenly I felt very angry and snatching my arm away from him I hissed "I am not a bloody child! Do not speak to me like that! And do not shout at me!" Throwing the secateurs on to the ground in an act of defiance I continued "If I am a prisoner and have to stay in at all times then I wish that I had died in the sea, at least my soul would be free."

It was as if I had smacked Don in the face, he looked totally shocked by my outburst "Please don't say that I'm sorry for shouting it's just that when I saw that the house was empty I thought……" His voice trailed away as he swallowed hard "Anyway there are things that we need to discuss, so if you don't mind would you please come back indoors." With that he turned and briskly walked towards the open back door.

Like a petulant child I slowly followed him back into the house. Once inside I made myself comfortable on the big squashy sofa, that stood in the middle of the sitting room, and listened as he bustled about in the kitchen making coffee. Once he was seated he looked at me and I could see that something was troubling him. "What is it? Has something happened to Suzie?"

"No, no" he handed me a cup of steaming coffee, "as you know we need the cartel to think that you did indeed die at sea and we have to make the situation seem as believable as possible." He stopped and I could see that he was trying to decide how to word his next statement "your house in Somerset needs to be sold and Margaret needs to think that you are in fact dead!"

I thought that my heart was going to stop "No" I realised that I had shouted this, so lowering my voice "please Don, there must be another way. I love that house. Why do we have to lie to Margaret? I can't bear the thought of her going through the pain of grieving for me when I'm still alive!"

Moving to sit next to me, he takes my hand in his "I'm sorry, truly I am but there is no other way. We have to do everything that would normally be undertaken on someone's death." He looks down at his hands that are resting on his knees and added "if the cartel gets wind that you are still alive we don't know what they will do. Margaret if the person closes to you and our intelligence officers are concerned that if the cartel gets suspicious they may kidnap Margaret to try to flush you out of hiding." A sudden sob that escapes from my lips brings his eyes back up to my face, "you have to realise that these people will stop at nothing to get Jose and Pablo out of prison. I'm sorry but you have to understand that to all intents and purposes Polly Oakley is dead! And you are now and forever will be known as Christina Burton."

The next few days were surreal as Don informed the local police station in Somerset, that I had been killed in a dreadful boating accident in the Caribbean and that due to the fact that the boat had, unfortunately, exploded that there would be no body to bring home. He had asked that one of their more sympathetic detectives should be sent to break the terrible news to Margaret.

Once she had been told, Don had sent one of my 'nieces' along with a 'nephew' down to Somerset to meet Margaret at the house. The told her that they were solicitors acting in connection with my instructions on my Will. They asked her if she would like any of my personal possessions. They led her to believe that the proceeds of the furniture and house sell, along with my personal wealth, had been left to charity, so stated that if there was anything that she wanted she needed to take it immediately. I was not allowed to keep anything, not even my mothers jewellery or my fathers pocket watch, so I was glad to hear that Margaret had asked for these items. It was arranged that a house clearance company removed all of the furniture and the house was put on the market.

The very next week Don received news from 'the solicitors' that a very substantial cash offer had been received for my beautiful Somerset home and that the sale process would now start. We were sitting at the big wooden kitchen table when Don broke the news to me. "But what am I to do? I can't stay hidden away forever" I suddenly felt bereft "my whole life cannot consist of hiding and being afraid all of the time."

"The cartel will only keep looking for you if there is a chance that you are still alive." For the first time he was unable to look me in the eye, something seemed to be bothering him.

"Don, what is it? There's something that you're not telling me!" looking at his face, deep down I knew that whatever the problem it must be big. "Tell me!"

Keeping his eyes firmly fixed on the wooden tabletop he started to speak "We have intelligence that two suspect members of the cartel are about to enter the country, they are in fact in transit as we speak. Due to this I cannot be seen here."

"The cartel still think of me as part of the team, remember I supplied the men for the 'yacht parties' and was heavily involved with setting up the London shop. Our intelligence think that once the men arrive they will want to make contact with me." I could tell from his expression that he was very troubled "if they don't believe me when I tell them that all I have hear is that you died in mysterious circumstances then they might decide to follow me. We can't chance that happening."

"Don, will this ever be over?" I tried to sound calm, but my voice gave me away and as I spoke the trembling spread from my voice throughout my whole body. "I don't want to be here on my own!"

At last, he looked at me, "Do you remember the last time that you flew into Barbados, there was a man who engaged you in conversation?" After everything that had happened over the last few months that man had become irrelevant to me, but I did remember him. "Well, he's one of our finest officers and he will be coming down to stay with you, in fact he should be arriving at any time. I trust him implicitly and have no concern about leaving you in his capable hands." Don looked at his watch and frowned "In fact he's late, I need to get going soon, as I must be back in London before their flight lands."

As if on cue we heard the crunch of gravel, which heralded the arrival of a vehicle. Don jumped up and standing to one side of the kitchen window, peeped out between the slats of the blind in the direction of the driveway. Once he was satisfied that it was the person he was waiting for he made his way to the front door. I heard the murmur of voices, but was unable to hear what they were saying.

Chapter 22

Over the next couple of day Joe and I settled into a routine, he would go out early for a jog and then on his way back to the house he would call into the little shop at the bottom of the road and bring back an armful of daily newspapers. We would then scour each one for any mention of the impending drug trial. Day after day that was nothing until suddenly "Oh, dear God" was all I could say, as I stared at a picture of Suzie, looking wild eyed and frightened. She was in what looked like a courtroom and was seated between two very burly female prison officers. The headline seemed to jump off the page at me 'Middle Aged British Woman Held in Drug Bust' I couldn't bear to look at her face any longer and pushed the paper across the table to Joe.

Silently he started to read the article, but after a while he looked up and said "I think that you should hear this" with that he started to read…….

It is stated by the Barbados authorities that Suzie Gilbert, a middle-aged woman from Dorset, who emigrated to Barbados a number of years ago, is believed to be one of the main ringleaders in a major organisation that has been trafficking drugs into the UK. She along with her associates Jose Escodracon and Pablo Cortenda have been, for the last year, smuggling cocaine into Britain under the disguise of dresses that have been sold via a shop called 'Heaven Sent' in London.

The London arm of the organisation is believed to have been set up and run by Ms Gilbert's long-time friend Mrs Polly Oakley. However, it has been stated in court by the defendant that Mrs Oakley either fell or was pushed overboard during one of the infamous yacht parties. Her body has never been found.

Ms Gilbert, is also accused of running a prostitution ring, supplying young girls for wealthy men at the aforementioned yacht parties.

The case against the three defendants continues.

"Joe, do you think that this means that I am safe? I mean if they are acknowledging in court that I'm dead, will they still be looking for me?" I try to read his face for any reaction, when a sudden thought strikes me "Oh god, will I be put on trial here? They said that I am the London arm for this, so will I be held responsible?" I honestly think at that moment that I must be going crazy.

To my surprise Joe starts to laugh "How can you be held responsible if your dead!" Leaning forward he puts his hands flat on the tabletop, "I understand what you mean, but there is no possibility of you going to prison. You were coerced by us to join the organisation; you were unaware of why it was important for you to be involved. We needed someone who was totally oblivious to what Suzie and her associates were up to. When you turned up out of the blue in Barbados a total innocent, the plan came together.

"So, are you telling me that all of my time spent in Barbados, and with Don, has been a sham?" For some reason, I felt totally let down by Don, had he just been play acting all of the time, making out that he liked me just so that he could bring Suzie down!

"We made sure that someone was close to you at all times, looking out for you." He didn't seem to want to look at me and swallowing hard he added "although that last night…."

"Yes, what about the last night! I get thrown in the sea and left to die so where was the person who should have been close to me, watching out for me?" I knew that it wasn't Joe's fault but he was the only one there, "so come on, what happened on the last bloody night, who allowed me to be thrown into the sea and left me thinking that I was going to die in the bloody cold ocean!"

"Our intelligence told us that Suzie was going to meet Jose and Pablo, there was no mention of you." At last, he looked at me, "when Honey asked where you were I thought that Don was going to go crazy. I've never in the of my years that I've worked with him seen him like that!" Drumming his fingers on the table he went on "When Suzie was asked and she just pointed out to sea, I honestly thought that he was going to hit her. At first light he sent up a police helicopter and organised boats to search for you." Looking down he hesitated "I'm sorry to tell you, but Suzie sent us in the wrong direction. It wasn't until we spoke to the girls again, that Chantelle mentioned that the yacht had been heading towards St Lucia, it was then that we realised that the search was taking place miles from where you had been left."

I couldn't stop the tears from flowing "Why would she do that?" I spluttered between sobs "we've know each other for years. I held her when her parents passed away, we have been such good friends. Why would she want me dead?"

"She was travelling in a different world from yours for a number of years, when you mix with that type of person you have to become hard!" he spoke in a soft voice "sometimes they get caught up in all of it, and somehow none of it seems real anymore. It's as though they are watching a movie and can just turn it off and carry on as normal." He stood and walked over to the drinks cabinet, he selected two glasses and a bottle of brandy, "it might be a bit early for this but I think that you need it." Without turning to face me he pushed a glass of the amber liquid across the table in my direction and continued to speak. "The friend that you knew in England has been swallowed up with greed of both money and status" when I make no comment he added "Christina, think about this, can you remember how much you were paid just for being a chaperone at the yacht party? If I remember rightly Don said that it was about $5000" I nodded to confirm this "from working with the girls alone, Suzie would have become a millionaire. The problem is money breeds greed for more money and that's how she got tangled up with the cartel. If she had stayed as a 'madam' she would, most probably, still be free instead of facing a possible life sentence."

"Bloody hell, LIFE!" I hadn't considered until now how long she would get.

"Christina, you must be prepared to hear the worst. If the Barbados criminal system feels that Suzie had any part in you 'falling' overboard…" he stopped and looked straight into my eyes "it could mean a death sentence!"

At that moment I felt as though the room was moving and I gripped the edge of the heavy table to try to steady myself, rubbing my hand over my face "I suppose that's what they did to me when they left me there….." big fat tears were now rolling down my face and landing with a plop on the table "as fish food!"

Chapter 23

Later that week Joe received a call from London, saying that he was needed back in the city for a few days and that a female officer would be coming down to stay with me. For some reason I felt really uneasy. Crossing my arms over my chest I asked him "Joe, was that Don?"

"No, it was dispatch calling on his behalf." As he spoke he continued to gather a few things that he would need to take with him.

"But Joe, Don said that it would always be him that called if our instructions needed to change." My stomach was starting to do somersaults "do you think that you should call him back, just to check?"

"I really think that you're becoming paranoid. How would they have got my number if Don hadn't given it to them. Don's the only one that has this number." He clicked the locks shut on his case "don't worry, everything is alright!"

But I did worry. Something just didn't feel right. Don had specifically said that I would always have his best male officers with me. I know that it's not politically correct, but he felt that should the cartel show up that a male officer would be better equipped to deal with the situation. Something very definitely did not seem or feel right.

About an hour later a small dark coloured car pulled into the driveway. Joe gave me a hug and told me not to worry, with that he strolled out of the front door and walked across the drive towards the young woman, who was getting out of the car. For a few brief moments they talked and then on a shake of hands Joe got into his car and he was gone.

Peering out from behind the kitchen blinds I felt that there was something familiar about this young woman, but I couldn't think why. As I watched, she had walked around to the back of her car and had taken a suitcase out of the car boot and was now pulling it across the gravel driveway towards the house. On entering, I was surprised that she didn't bother to call out but walked straight through to the kitchen area.

On closer inspection I saw that she was of medium height and build. Her hair was cut in a very sever bob and had been dyed raven black, the colour made her already pale skin look ghostly white. It seemed odd to me that Don would send such a petite officer for protection, especially as he had information that members of the cartel were in England. I pushed the thought to the back of my mind. I concentrated on the fact that Joe must have been satisfied otherwise he wouldn't have left me alone here with her.

"Do I hear a kettle boiling?" She had a soft northern accent and again I was sure that I had heard that voice somewhere in the past.

"Are you hungry?" I politely asked.

"Bacon butty, would go down a treat." I noticed that she didn't say please and this rankled me a little. "Which room is mine?" But before I could answer she had walked back out of the kitchen and was heading for the staircase "don't worry, I'll find it." She shouted over her shoulder.

This dreadful uneasiness was starting to creep from my stomach all over my body and I tried to rack my brains where and when I had met this girl before but try as I might nothing sprung to mind.

The rest of the evening was spent, for the most part, in silence. I had tried to make conversation with her over supper but she had made it obvious that she wasn't interested in small talk.

Just after 10.00 pm the girl, now know as Emma, locked the downstairs windows and doors. To my surprise she put the keys in her trousers pocket, when she saw me watching her she said, "I'll take care of these, we don't want any intruders, do we?"

In the early hours of morning a sudden noise coming from the kitchen, which was immediately under my bedroom, woke me. I wasn't sure what to do and for a few moments lay there quietly listening to the sounds of movements, that could clearly be heard through the old floorboards. Silently I got out of bed and crept out of my room making my way, as quietly as the floorboards would let me, to Emma's room. On reaching her door I hesitate, should I knock or just walk in. As I reached out towards the door handle a hand clamped down over my mouth and my head was violently jerked back into someone's body.

"Well, Mrs Nosy what are you doing creeping around at this time of the morning?" the hand seemed to tighten across my mouth as the person spoke "now that you're up you can have my little surprise earlier than I had anticipated." The sleep suddenly cleared from my brain and I recognised Emma's voice, "I'm going to take my hand away from your mouth, but as you already know, it's not a bit of good you screaming because there's no-one hear to help you." As she spoke she pushed me towards the staircase "now get down there!"

On entering the kitchen I couldn't believe my eyes, on the table she had laid out syringes, a couple of spoons and some little bags of white powder. "Welcome to your house of fun!" With that she forcefully pushed me towards a chair that had been placed in the middle of the kitchen floor.

As I was slammed onto the big wooden chair, I finally came face to face with her, a shudder coursed through my body. A mass of mousy coloured curls had taken the place of the sever black bob, that she had arrived with, her hair now reminded me of my own, before it had been dyed a deep auburn.

I now knew where I had seen her before, "You're the one off of the plane?" When she didn't reply but just stood there looking at me, "but Don said that you were to have nothing to do with me" a light bulb seemed to suddenly click on in my brain "the phone call……" before I could finish what I was about to say, she struck me hard across the face. As I reeled from the shock she started to roughly tie me to the chair with a thick coarse rope, that had been stored under the kitchen table.

"Shut up, you stupid cow." Her voice was pure evil, it reminded me of the one's that you hear on the detective programs on the TV, when the murderer is caught. "If Joe is so stupid not to check, who's fault is that!" She turned away from me and started to do something with the items on the table.

"If you're going to kill me, you could at least tell me why?" I tried not to sound frightened, even though I knew that my end was most probably very close.

Turning her face to look at me she hissed "Kill you! You're a good few hours away from meeting your maker, no we're going to have some fun first." With that she picked up one of the packets of white powder. "But I will tell you why you are going to die. You see this?" She shook that packet in my face "this is what you and your friends killed my brother with!"

"I haven't killed anyone." I tried to plead with her "I don't even know what that is!"

"I don't even know what that is," she mimicked me in a silly whiny voice "this you stupid fucking cow is Cocaine, Coke, Blow, Big C, Snow or any other fucking name you want to call it!" I noticed as she spoke that she had balled her fist around the bag of powder and for a moment I thought that she was about to hit me again. "This is what killed my little brother Harry and this is what will kill you …" she paused and with a stupid smirk on the face spat out the last word "   EVENTUALLY." She seemed to be contemplating her next move "killing people is exhausting work, so I think a really good breakfast is called for before I start!" Was my mind already playing tricks on me, was she really going to have breakfast!

As I sat tied to the chair, everything seemed surreal, sitting there watching, my would be murderer, whilst she bustled about the kitchen, cooking bacon and eggs and making coffee, to an outsider the situation would seem ridiculous like something out of a bad movie.

As she sat down at the table to enjoy her meal, my mind started to work through the events of the previous day. Surely if Don had not called Joe bask to London someone would soon arrive to save me. However, I worked out that he wouldn't have got back to the city in time to meet Don yesterday as it would have been well after 8.00 pm. I'm sure that as soon as he walks into the office this morning that all hell will break loose.

Arching my back, I try to see the kitchen clock, but it's just out of view. Looking out of the window I can see that the sun is coming up, it's still far too early for them to have realised what has happened. I know that there is no way that she will hold off from hurting me for a least another 3 hours. I have to try to think of a way to stall her, at least to give them time to try and get here to save me.

The scrapping of chair legs on the stone kitchen floor brings me back to reality. What can I do to stop this insanity? Perhaps if I can get her to think about the consequences of her actions, she might come to her senses.

My voice as I start to speak seems to startle her, "I know that you are going to kill me, but have you thought about what will happen to you?" again she just stares at me "have you thought how this will affect your family?" I push on "After all your parents have already lost their son!"

"Shut your filthy mouth!" before I knew what was happening she has leapt across the kitchen table and is standing in front of me, her breakfast knife still firmly in her hand, "don't you dare talk about my family with your filthy mouth!" With that she slashes the knife across my cheek, drawing back from she mutters "next time it will be your throat!"

The pain of the knife cutting through my flesh made me reel in shock, I could feel the blood trickling down my face and onto my neck to be soaked up by my dressing gown collar. As she drew back as if to slash me for a second time with the knife, something suddenly makes her stop. Cocking her head to one side she seemed to be listening intently, without another word she swiftly moved across the room to the window overlooking the back garden. Positioning herself to one side of the large window and making sure that she was hidden by the heavy curtains, she peers out as if waiting for something to happen.

A sudden noise from the side of the house makes her spring into action, reaching under her jumper she pulls out a small gun from the waistband of her jeans. Quickly she moves towards the side door, that leads out into the garden. From my position I can just see the back of her as she crouches down and silently opens the door.

For a moment everything is quiet until a distant sound breaks through the early morning air. Straining my ears to make out the sound I realise that the noise is the sound of a helicopter and I start to pray that it's Don coming to rescue me.

My prayers are stopped by a man's voice shouting just outside of the kitchen window "Traidor debes morir como un perro!" this is followed by rapid gun fire. After that everything goes eerily quiet.

Sitting tied to the chair, I know that if that man comes inside the house, that I won't stand a chance. I start to try to untie the huge knot in the rope but it is impossible, the circulation in my hands has been cut off for too long and my fingers just won't work.

The familiar sound of tyres on the gravel driveway makes me ridged with fear. I can hear the sound of heavy boots running towards the house and the front door being kicked in, the voices in the hallway are getting nearer, please God let them kill me quickly. I close my eyes and await my fat.

Chapter 24

Later Don told me that Emma had died from a single gun shot on her way to the hospital. A note had been stuffed in her mouth which read 'Traidor, debes morir como un perro'. One of Don's intelligence officers had roughly translated this as 'Traitor, you must die like a dog." The officer confirmed that this was the Columbus Cartels motto. I told Don that I had heard this being shouted immediately before the shots had been fired.

My heart broke for Emma's parents and I wondered, and still do, how they coped with the news that their child had been shot in such an awful way. Don tried to reassure me that they would have been given a completely different scenario regarding her death. As it couldn't be revealed that it was a police officer shot dead and not me.

The intelligence officer had told Don that they believed that two members of the cartel had followed Emma, after seeing her leave headquarters with a suitcase. The intelligence officer said that they believe that the two cartel members, would have hoped that Emma would either have information about my death or if I was still alive know where I was being hidden.

When she walked out of the house on that fateful morning, they must have believed that it was me. Any photo that they would have seen would have shown a lady with curly mousy hair, different from the way that they would have seen Emma who had arrived with a short dark bob.

Don pointed out that the only good thing that had come out of this situation was that the cartel would now be convinced that I was dead!

It was two years later when news reached us that Suzie's trial was finally over. All three of them, Suzie, Jose and Pablo had been sentenced to life imprisonment without the possibility of parole, for their part in the setting up of the organisation and of the smuggling of cocaine. Other lesser members of the organisation were given sentences ranging from three to ten years.

Suzie was also charged with being a 'madam' encouraging girls into prostitution and supplying them for the men at the yacht parties.

No-one was ever charged with my murder!

Printed in Great Britain
by Amazon